ALL'S FAIR IN PUCKS AND WAR

RUSH HOCKEY #5

ELISE FABER

ALL'S FAIR IN PUCKS AND WAR
BY ELISE FABER

Newsletter sign-up

Rush Hockey

Big Puck Energy
Filthy Puckboy
So Pucking Over It
Love, Pucks, and Other Stories
All's Fair in Pucks and War
No Pucks Lost Between Us

PROLOGUE

BILLIE ROSE

I stared out at my town—whole and yet different.

A phoenix from the ashes that had been reborn.

Lights twinkled in the distance. The stars sparkled overhead. The moon's glow was muted by a transparent swathe of clouds.

It was otherworldly.

And peaceful.

Except for the fact that I was sitting on the hillside outside of town, hating my life.

Because...my heart was broken.

Because I had trusted someone to take care with it.

A mistake.

I'd made it.

In believing I was *Joel's*. That he was mine.

The man I loved. The life, the *home* I'd finally gotten to create, to be part of, to hold close to my heart...was a fucking sham.

A lie.

A—

My lungs hitched, tears filling my eyes, clinging to my lashes, then dripping down my cheeks.

Joel Marshall. Hockey player. Quote-unquote nice guy.

Liar.

Cheater.

Heartbreaker.

ONE

BILLIE ROSE

I sighed, rolled over in the back of my little SUV, and stared through the moonroof, my eyes on the dark sky, on the stars and clouds and the glow of the moon.

My tears had dried.

But the gaping crevice in my chest ached and throbbed and *burned*.

That acid scorched through every cell and nerve, eyes to heart to toes.

The man I loved, who I thought was the other half of my soul...

Was married.

To a gorgeous blonde with curves for days and no pores on her face and perfect winged liner.

On both eyes!

Not one curved up and the other a little flat.

Not one big and the other—

"Enough about her eyeliner, Billie," I muttered to myself, pushing up from where I'd laid the seats out flat, up from the blankets and pillows I'd placed beneath me so I wouldn't wake up in the morning with a back that told me exactly how close I was getting to thirty.

Too close.

I slid out from the back of my SUV, away from a space I'd slept in far too many times before—

That crevice in my chest rattled, an earthquake sending shards of rock down the sides, threatening collapse...until, ultimately, it just grew wider.

Because he'd pursued—*actively pursued*—me.

Despite every roadblock and wall I'd erected to keep him at a distance, despite the moat I'd dug and filled with razor wire and radioactive sharks with freaking laser beams on their heads, despite the way I used work to shore up every part of my worth, Joel had pursued me.

And the man had deliberately torn down and paved over and scheduled away with custom stickers and washi tape each and every barrier between my heart and the outside world.

He'd made me feel loved and valued and wanted.

He'd paid attention.

He'd *shown* me love.

With time and care and paying attention. With washi tape and stickers and soft words and—

My eyes filled with tears again, throat closing up, lungs hitching.

"Fuck you, Joel," I gritted out, swiping at the hot beads of moisture dripping down my cheeks. "Just. Fuck. *You!*" I shouted, reaching back into my trunk and grabbing my planning bag. I shoved my hand inside the thick canvas, grasping at the contents.

For what had been a prized possession I'd hoarded so damned carefully.

Now—as my fingers closed around the roll of washi tape—I knew it was all bullshit.

I yanked the tape out, printed with scenes from the local NHL team, the San Francisco Gold, along with a newer one he'd ordered. This one was printed with the logo and colors of the Gold's their minor league affiliate, the Rush—the actual team Joel played for—and—

"Fuck you," I whispered, winding up, the ring of reusable tape held tight in my hand, and letting my arm swing forward.

Stopping, fingers clenched tight.

Unable to let it go.

"Stupid. Stupid. *Stupid*." I shoved my curls out of my face. "He's *married*."

And *not* to me.

Even though I loved him.

Even though fantasies of me in a white dress, holding a wildflower bouquet, had begun to cling to the edges of my mind. Even though I'd practically had an orgasm thinking about all the ways I could tackle a seating chart.

The spreadsheets I could make.

Chef's kiss.

Maybe it was the grief of those lost spreadsheets, or maybe it was the anger welling up again, making me feel like a complete and total idiot.

Grief and anger often felt very similar.

And God knew I'd had more than my fair share in my life.

Maybe that was why the second time I wound up, the second time I allowed my arm to fly forward, my fingers opened and the roll of custom washi tape flew over the edge of the parking lot, lost somewhere down the hill I'd backed up to, disappearing into the dark of the night.

And it was followed by the next and the next and the *next*.

Until there was no trace of Joel.

Of my stupidity.

Of my mistake.

At least until my fingers brushed the edge of my sticker book and my breath hitched again and—

The stickers.

The ones Joel had made for me. Sheets of cartoon versions of us smiling and hugging and kissing and—

That crevice in my chest shook.

My heart convulsed.

"Fuck you, Joel," I whispered and yanked out the sheet...

Just as gravel crunched.

I spun, stomach clenching.

I was on the fucking side of a mountain, trying to get my mind together, trying to fill in that damned crevice—no matter how futile I knew my attempts would be. But mostly, I was on the side of this fucking mountain because I wanted to avoid *this*.

Because only one person knew I came here.

Slept here.

And I'd...

I guess I hoped he'd have been too busy with that wife of his to come looking for me.

Rocks were kicked up, the sound of the car's motor grew louder, headlights flashed...and then Joel's car was pulling in next to me, heat from the engine hitting my ankles before it shut off.

The driver's side door opened.

My fingers clenched on the sheet of stickers, crumpling one corner, scrunching up my cartoon face.

Making it so the other version of myself looked like a maniacal villain.

Either that or like a crumpling heroine, sobs wracking her frame.

Which...was so not what I wanted to be thinking about.

Not with Joel unfolding out of his car, his big, tall body sending a bolt of heat through me, making my pulse speed up, my insides brace, and—

"Rosie," he said.

I shivered.

"What the fuck are you doing?" A rasping, annoyed question.

What the fuck are you doing?

What. The. Fuck. Are—

"What the fuck am *I* doing?" I snapped, balling up the stickers, crunching our faces, the cute planners and pucks and borders, the rage burning in my belly making any fucks I had to give about ruining the planning product poof off into nothing. "*What the fuck am I doing?!*"

Was I yelling?

Um, yes.

Did I give a fuck?

Yeah, no.

This man had a wife at home—a goddamned *wife*—and he was asking *me* what the—

"Rosie," he murmured, coming close.

He smelled good.

Why did he smell good?

"Don't touch me," I snapped, lurching back from him.

He didn't listen, just reached for my hand, the closest of which held that crumpled sheet of stickers.

I jerked it back, but he was a professional hockey player.

He was big and strong and...fast.

He caught my hand, slipped the paper from my fist.

Froze.

A sigh, his eyes coming to mine, deep pools of emerald in the dark of the night. I watched as he carefully smoothed out the sticker paper, just as carefully folded it, and slipped it into his pocket. "Rosie."

I flinched. He sounded like I felt, hurt and broken and—

He had a *wife*.

I turned away, moving to the trunk of my SUV, hitching my planner bag onto my shoulder and slamming the hatch closed.

"Sweetheart."

"No," I said. "No, Joel. Just...*no.*" I shoved my hand into my bag, searched for the keys.

Except, I found another roll of washi.

Christ.

"Rosie, baby, just stop for a second and—"

I chucked the roll at his head.

And missed by a mile, sending it rolling down the hill to join its brethren in the graveyard of tape below.

"What the fuck?" he snapped.

I stormed over to him, jabbed a finger into his chest. "You. Have. A. Wife." The hand that was in my bag closed in on another of Joel's stickers and I yanked out the sheet, shoving it in his face. "You made these! You made a place for me in your life and fucking shoved yourself into mine, cemented yourself into my heart a-and you have a *fucking wife!*"

I was shouting.

Screaming, really.

Spittle flying. Tears streaming. The sticker sheet scrunched up and sailing over the edge.

My hand went back into my bag, fingers finally finding my keys.

Time to go.

To run.

To piece myself together.

I yanked the key fob out, started to turn away. "I'll be in contact to get my stuff—"

Joel snatched my keys out of my hand.

They were there and gone as quickly as that sheet of stickers had been.

But he didn't carefully slide my keys into his pocket.

The fob didn't join the stickers.

Nope.

My keys joined the graveyard of washi tape as Joel reared back and threw them over the side of the hill.

Two

JOEL

Normally, I loved getting a step up on Billie.

Making her sputter, seeing her expression transform with shock.

But this was pretty much the worst-case scenario.

It was day one—day *fucking* one—of the rest of our lives together and I'd come home to find Willow sitting in my fucking living room.

On my couch.

And Billie gone.

Not in the apartment we'd just moved into together, not at City Hall.

Not at the rink.

Not at Bailey's ranch, the rebuild complete.

Not at Monroe's with Dessie, sipping on a glass of wine.

Nowhere.

But Willow was.

Willow. *Fuck*. Five years since I'd seen my ex.

Five years without a fucking word.

And now Billie was talking about a wife.

Which didn't make any fucking sense. Five years. Five fucking years and—

"What are you doing?" Billie shouted, her body slamming up against mine, as though she could stop me from sending my arm forward. Even though I'd already finished the movement and she had no hope of halting me.

"Tell me what happened," I said, extracting my arm from her grip, slipping my hand into my pocket, opening my fist.

My Rosie narrowed her eyes, stepping back, putting several feet between us. "You mean with your wife?"

Wife again.

When that didn't make any sense.

When Willow should be my *ex*-wife.

When five years had passed and—

"Yeah," she muttered when I didn't immediately answer, shaking her head and turning away. "That's exactly what I thought."

I didn't even know *what* to think. Willow had been there on my couch and Billie had been gone, and I'd spent the last hours searching for the woman I loved and—

Rosie yanked open the driver's side door on her SUV, dumping her bag into the passenger's seat and then bending, giving me a glimpse of tight black leggings covering a lush ass that I'd fucked, that I'd kissed and stroked and held on to as I pounded into her sweet, tight cunt.

Plastic creaked, and I snapped out of it, moving over to her.

"What are you doing?"

Her body went stiff, but she didn't answer me.

"Rosie baby," I murmured, daring to place a gentle hand on her back as she bent and studied something beneath the steering wheel.

Her muscles flexed beneath my palm, going even stiffer under my touch, but I didn't back away.

"What are you doing, sweetheart?" I pressed.

Still no answer.

So, I leaned closer, soaked in the scent of her, the feel of her, the fact that I'd found her and she was safe and—

"*Oof!*" I grunted when her elbow collided with my gut, sending my lungs wheezing, my muscles protesting. "Not nice, Rosie baby," I grumbled, rubbing my belly.

"I can tell you something else that's *not nice*," she muttered, still working at whatever was in front of her.

Before she could dive deeper on the *not nice* part of the evening, I asked again, "What are you doing?"

She was still bent, elbow resting on the seat, hands working, head tucked beneath the steering wheel as the plastic continued to creak and groan.

A curse, one that the guys on the team would approve of. "None of your business."

"Just saying, I could help you with—"

Whirling—and just narrowly missing cracking her head on the steering wheel, something that had me jerking forward, hand extending as though I could shield her from the impact—

Then she was in my face again, hands on my chest, but where normally they would have flattened, would have slid up to cup my shoulders, to serve as a rest for her weight as she rose on tiptoe, brushed her mouth over mine, my Billie Rose shoved me.

Hard.

"Help me?" she snapped, eyes flashing. "*Help* me? *You're* going to help *me?*"

Her lips were parted and if it was daytime, the sun illuminating her face instead of just the overhead lights in her car, I knew her cheeks would have been flushed with rage, a bright pink that reminded me of her moaning my name, her skin flushed for a whole different reason.

One a lot more pleasurable than an argument under the stars.

Than hurt in pretty blue darkened to navy under the midnight sky.

"Yeah," I murmured, "I want to help you."

She huffed out another breath, turned back to the space below her steering wheel. "You can start by leaving."

Yeah, that wasn't happening.

"I can't do that."

Her head dropped, forehead hitting the leather of that front seat. "Then you can *start* by telling me why you have a wife, Joel."

"I don't have a wife." I *shouldn't* have a wife.

Billie turned around again, this time slower and with eyes that were still midnight—only not from anger, but from sadness.

I'd made her sad.

When I'd promised myself her days would only be filled with happiness.

Her voice was quiet. "Then why did she introduce herself as your wife, Joel?"

I didn't fucking know. But...how exactly did I explain that I'd signed papers and now my ex was in town claiming she was still my wife and—

None of it made any sense.

"I don't know, Rosie."

She flinched.

Like she used to. Like I'd called her harpy and sliced her deep without meaning to and—

"I left her on your couch," Billie said softly. "I left her on the couch we picked out together, her back propped up by one of *my* throw pillows, a cup of coffee in her hand." Her lips pressed flat. Released on a sigh. "I left her there so you two could talk and—"

"No," I said. "You left so you could run. You *left* because that's your first inclination when any sort of bump appears in a relationship. You left because you're hurt and—"

She threw up her hands. "You're fucking married!"

My chest went tight, pain lancing through my middle. Had we

really been through all we'd been through—enemies to tentative acquaintances to friends to lovers to *everything*—and we were right back here?

Billie Rose throwing up walls.

Running.

I got that Willow was a shock.

Hell, it was a shock for *me*. That chapter of my fucking life was supposed to be closed. Willow had dumped me, divorced my ass, and moved on.

I hadn't contested a thing.

Just signed papers and a check and went on with my life.

"Her being on my couch with one of your *many* throw pillows behind her back isn't exactly what I expected to walk into when I got home from practice," I said.

She snorted. "Yeah, I bet. Since that means your house of lies is tumbling down."

"Lies?" I snapped, hurt now overwhelmed by anger. I was tired, had been tired when I got home from practice, but I was fucking exhausted now. The shock of Willow, making sure she was good before I told her I couldn't do whatever the fuck she needed to do because Billie was gone.

Because she'd been there and gotten that cup of coffee for my ex-fucking-wife.

And then had gone.

And that hadn't been good. It had been *disastrous*.

I'd known in my belly, my bones.

But I *hadn't* known it had been *this*. That she'd assume, that she wouldn't talk to me, that we were right back *here*.

Again.

And I was tired.

I'd worked my ass off to prove—

"Yes." She poked me in the chest again. "You're a liar, Joel Marshall. A big, fucking liar who couldn't help me even if I wanted you to." She crossed her arms. "Which I don't. Because I can hot-wire my own damned car."

Hot-wire? Christ. She was *that* desperate to be away from me?

One look at her face gave me my answer.

I sighed.

She huffed.

But still, I swallowed my temper and tried again. "I don't have a wife."

She turned her head away.

"I need you to trust me, sweetheart," I said gently. "Just take a breath. Think about me. About us, and...just trust me."

THREE

BILLIE ROSE

"And...just trust me."

Trust him?

Trust him?

How the fuck could I trust a man whose wife had just knocked on his front door? A gorgeous, beautiful, model-like wife who fit the gorgeous hockey player towering over me a hell of a lot better than I did.

How could I trust a man who was out of my league?

How could I trust that his feelings for me were real?

How could I trust that what we were building meant as much to him as it did to me?

Because it could just as easily be a lie. Or even if not a *malicious* lie, just...something that wasn't as important to him.

I couldn't be as important to him.

It just wasn't...

It just wasn't possible. I was the one who did the work, who cared more, who—

Joel's shoulders slumped, and he looked away, throat working.

"I don't know what's happening," he whispered. "I don't know what's happening, but I'll figure it out and it'll be okay. I'll make it okay." He glanced over his shoulder, gaze colliding with mine. "I just need you to trust me."

I clenched my hands into fists, wanting to touch him again, but not to shove or poke or push him over the hill into the dark brush below. I wanted to stroke my fingers through his beard. I wanted to hold him close. I wanted to cup his face in my hands, pull him to me, and tell him that everything was going to be okay.

Except...he had a wife.

So, instead of stepping toward him and taking him in my arms, instead of patching up the crevice in my chest, I let it grow wider.

I slid back a pace.

And immediately regretted it.

Because he was watching me, those deep green eyes focused on me.

So, he saw me retreat, saw that step back, saw the distance I allowed to grow between us, and *I* saw the way his face changed, hurt entering his eyes, his shoulders slumping further, and—

He looked away, staring out into the darkness.

Quiet.

Hurt.

I'd hurt him.

And seriously, what the fuck? How was *I* the bad guy here? *I* was the one who'd been wronged. I was the one who was hurt. I was the one who—

Joel spun toward me, so quickly that I stumbled back another step, that I found myself bumping into my door, the metal panel swinging shut with a *thunk*.

Then he was in my face, bending close, eyes flashing, brows drawn together into a tight furrow.

"Joel," I whispered.

He bent closer, hand coming to my hip. "I don't know what's

going on," he whispered. "I don't know why Willow's here or what she said to you—"

Willow.

Fuck, that fit the beautiful woman who'd been standing on the stoop, who I'd invited into Joel's apartment.

"She's your wife," I whispered.

A sharp shake of his head and he bent even closer, so close that I saw the individual hairs of his beard, coarse and dark with the odd strand of gray. I wanted to run my fingers through it, wanted to feel it brushing over my body, my naked skin, my neck as he kissed the hinge of my jaw. Spice in my nose, the masculine scent of him I knew better than my own perfume. The heat of his body sinking into mine, the cool evening air standing no chance when it came to this man.

"Trust me," he whispered.

My lips parted on an exhale and my fingers flexed, wanting to touch him.

Needing to. Just...not able to.

He straightened.

Jerked up. Jerked away from me.

Chipping away further at that crevice. Increasing the distance between us. Erecting *all* the barriers.

He turned his back on me, his big frame half-hidden in the mix of moonlight and shadows as he rounded the hood of his car and yanked open the driver's side door.

A flash of light illuminating him dropping into the seat.

Then gone again, the engine turning over, the reverse lights coming on as he backed out of the spot, gravel crunching under the tires as he turned for the exit, dust kicking up as he drove away.

Lights fading.

The noise quieting.

Until I was alone.

Again.

I sighed and turned back to my car. "Well, what are you going to do now?"

No keys.

No skill at hot-wiring, despite my lie to Joel. I could watch a YouTube video, could maybe make an attempt at twisting some wires together and starting my car up like people did in the movies. *If* I could get the plastic panel open that I'd been struggling with, scrabbling my nails over, trying to pop the corner up.

If the panel I was working so hard at opening was even the correct panel, was the one that had those wires I was supposed to twist together and—

Okay, I had to face it.

I wasn't going to be hot-wiring a car that evening.

More than likely, I'd blow something up, and we were still in a drought. With my luck I'd spark the dry underbrush, the plants would act like tinder, and then I'd be the cause of a fire.

Another fire.

Not that I was the cause of the first one.

That particular slice of crazy was currently awaiting trial, justice moving slower than the rebuild of our town that had been destroyed by the huge complex fire the previous year. A fire had been intentionally set, and it had taken lives, destroyed homes and memories and so much more.

I never wanted to go back to that, never wanted to risk it, however improbable.

I'd camp out.

And in the morning, I'd make a call.

I was Billie Rose. I was the mayor of River's Bend and I had superpowers. I had connections. I had the magical ability to get shit done, Mayoral Magic one might say.

I could make a phone call.

I could get a fucking ride.

But...that was going to come with questions I really didn't want to answer, the least of which was why I was parked out on the

Ridge, sleeping under the stars when I had just moved into a perfectly nice apartment with a perfectly nice hockey player who I should be cuddled up next to in our perfectly nice bed.

Either that or he should be coaxing me out of the office he'd made for me.

Lavender bookcases and two desks, storage boxes for my washi tape and stickers and dividers that I loved to decorate. Special paper, punches, stamps, pens that were heaven to write with, just gliding across the page with the most minimal of effort.

Joel should be moving into my space, shifting my hair aside, pressing a kiss to my nape, leaning in to murmur all sorts of naughty things in my ear.

Convincing me to pause work and go to bed.

And not really having to work too hard—or work at it at all. Because I was waiting for him, waiting for an excuse to leave my desk, and waiting for our time together.

To cuddle with the man I loved.

To kiss and hold and—

I sniffed, legs suddenly weak, vision going blurry, head throbbing.

Fingers shaking, I grasped at the handle, tugged open the driver's side door, and plunked my ass into the seat.

And froze.

Because something was jabbing me in my thigh.

My hand trembled as I reached into my pocket at my hip...

And felt the hard plastic of my key fob inside.

And remembered Joel leaning close, his hand resting on my side.

"He pretended," I whispered, fingers wrapping around my keys as I tugged them out, worry replaced with irritation...

Replaced with the narrowest blips of amusement.

He'd pretended to throw my keys over the edge.

Of course he had.

The Joel I knew wouldn't leave me stranded in the dark

without a way home, no matter how mad he was at me, no matter how we'd left things.

I sighed, held the keys tighter and stared up at the night sky, as though the stars might give me the answers I needed.

The Joel I knew...

The problem was that the Joel *I* knew wasn't married.

FOUR

JOEL

My eyes were burning, exhaustion in every single nerve ending and cell.

But mostly, my heart was heavy.

And didn't I sound like a poor, sad Eeyore?

Poor Joel Marshall, with a sad heart and a woman who didn't believe in him.

Poor Joe Marshall, who had a great family and a great life and a great career and great friends and a great woman—

Except not anymore.

Boo-hoo-hoo.

My life was so hard.

Pity party for one, sign me up.

I pulled into our assigned parking spot, trying to ignore the fact that it was empty, that normally I let Billie park there because I only got the one spot and I didn't want the woman I loved hauling her ass through the parking lot and up the stairs to our apartment early in the morning or late at night...or really at any time of day.

She wasn't coming back.

Definitely not that night.

Maybe not ever.

It had been hard as fuck for me to get through her walls before, to get her to give me a chance—and then a second one. But I wasn't sure I had it in me to go again. To fight. To battle for inches. To be shut down again and again and—

I sighed.

It didn't matter right then.

I needed sleep. I needed a clear head. And the latter would only happen if I got the former.

So bed. Putting Billie out of my mind for a few hours.

Regrouping and—

I'd gotten out of my car, was trudging up the steps to the apartment, eyes on the prize of the door and my bed inside.

Unfortunately, the prize was still out of reach.

Because Willow was sitting on the top step of the stairs.

Blocking my way to the apartment.

Keeping me from my bed.

I sighed, rocking to a stop three steps below her, watching as she scrambled to her feet, rubbing a hand over her face.

She'd done that when she was tired, trying to rub the sleep away.

Trying to stay up.

After I'd been on the road or at a game.

So unlike Billie, who was a force in and of herself, a never-ending well of energy, an Energizer Bunny who never seemed to run out of juice.

Willow was fragile. Soft. Almost weak.

Less my equal and more something I had to take care of.

Always.

And...I just didn't have that in me right now, didn't have the Billie Rose brand of zest for solving problems.

I. Was. Tired.

But this wasn't going away.

Willow wasn't going away.

She was standing in front of me, staring at me with those doe eyes and worried expression, and I knew I was in for a long night.

"Come on," I muttered, continuing up the stairs, turning to the side so I could move past her, could lead the way to the apartment I shared with Billie.

Then I unlocked the door and pushed inside.

She followed behind me.

Close behind me.

I ignored the way that made my nape crawl and moved into the kitchen, tugging open the fridge and snagging a beer.

Not offering one to Willow because I didn't want to extend this, didn't want to have this interaction go on longer than was necessary.

"Are you okay?" she asked, hovering in the doorway as I popped off the bottle cap and leaned back against the counter.

I took a long draw of my beer then just looked at her.

Was I okay?

How was anything about this possibly okay?

I sighed, plunked the bottle on the counter. "Do you want to start with telling me why the woman I love seems to think I have a wife?"

"I—" Teeth pressing into her bottom lip, her eyes skating away.

And, just like that, my stomach twisted.

Dropped.

Because I knew—fucking *knew*—that this wasn't going to be as simple as clearing up a misunderstanding, that this wasn't going to be a conversation that led to an easy solution. An actually hey-this-is-kind-of-funny story.

"What's going on, Willow?" I asked, resisting the urge to sigh again. "You wanted the divorce. You wanted to be done. *You* moved out and on and—" I grabbed my beer again, the contents inside sloshing around as I jerked it toward my mouth and took another long, fortifying guzzle. Trying for patience. Trying to come at this rationally.

When all I wanted to do was grab my ex—well, she was supposed to be my fucking *ex*—wife by the shoulders and shake her until she started making this situation make sense.

Unfortunately, this wasn't a hockey game.

I couldn't rattle the truth out of her with a hit, couldn't slash at her hands or the backs of her legs in warning, prompting her to get moving.

I couldn't get really pissed and shoot the puck right at her.

I had to wait for her to tell me the truth.

But all she did was stand in the doorway to my kitchen, her purse hitched on her shoulder, her teeth pressed into a red-painted bottom lip, and her weight shifting from foot to foot.

And I knew this was going to take a long fucking time.

There was a reason that we were divorced—or supposed to be, anyway.

We weren't compatible.

Willow hated conflict, would rather everything build up until a small problem became a crisis that threatened to implode instead of just talking it out in the first place.

I much preferred Billie's style of communication—up front.

Minus her whole running away tendency—in a lot of ways, she could communicate, could tell me exactly how she was thinking. But on the deeper shit, the stuff that was tough and we really had to work at, I still had to track those thoughts and emotions down, still had to corner her and coax it out of her, especially if whatever was going down made her feel vulnerable.

Which...damn, maybe I had a type.

I exhaled sharply, not wanting to think that deeply, not right then, not with Willow there.

She jumped.

"Willow," I said, striving for patience. "Talk to me."

Her eyes came to mine then drifted away again.

But she didn't fucking *speak*.

"Okay," I said, still striving for patience, albeit not finding it. "I'm going to ask you a series of yes and no questions, okay?"

Her throat worked, and I thought, for a moment, she wouldn't even answer that much.

But then she nodded, lip sliding free as she whispered. "Okay."

"Are we divorced?"

Hesitation, long enough that it gave me the answer that was already churning in my stomach.

But, to her credit, Willow answered. "No."

I knew it. I read that in her tone, her hesitation, and still, my lungs froze.

"Why?" I snapped. "I signed the fucking papers. I returned them to my lawyer. I—"

Her shoulders came up, and she froze again.

Right. I hadn't asked a yes-or-no question.

Breathe. Calm. "Are we still married?"

Not the best question, but the only yes-or-no query I could think of when I was on that razor's edge and my mind was spinning. What the fuck had happened? And *how* the fuck had it happened? And *why* the fuck was she here now, after all this time, when we were supposed to be divorced five years ago?

"Willow," I pressed, setting the beer down and moving toward her, ignoring the way her shoulders practically crept up to her ears.

Leaning close.

Meeting eyes I'd known intimately—every swirl of cerulean and navy and gray, every fleck of gold memorized—without having to stare into them, those pretty irises like a roadmap to my soul.

Or they'd once been, anyway.

"Yes," Willow finally whispered. "We're still married."

What. The. Fuck? Rage licked up my spine. But I held it together. *Barely*.

"How did this happen?" I rasped.

She glanced away, but I reached up, turned her face back to mine, forced her gaze to mine.

"How did this happen?" I asked again.

Those shoulders came up.

My patience wavered, but I clutched at it with my fingertips, managed to keep hold of it, and thank fucking *God*, but she began to talk.

"After you signed"—she nibbled at her bottom lip, released it —"I told your attorney we'd changed our minds."

"Changed our—"

I shook my head. Focused.

"What the fuck, Willow?"

FIVE

BILLIE ROSE

River's Bend was a small town.

A small town that had been in the news a lot—mostly because I'd spent a lot of time and energy putting us there, spotlighting climate change issues and funding concerns and scumbags at insurance companies.

So, we were known for that now—a fire and a fight to rebuild.

But the fire had destroyed everything, houses and pets and lives and historic buildings and businesses and natural California ecosystems (though an argument *could* be made that California had been designed to burn, some of the native redwoods only able to reproduce when their cones burned, opened, and released seeds for the baby giant conifers).

But fire was a problem, one increasingly dangerous year after year with changing weather patterns and a growing population that was living in burn zones and—

That was more than enough of my rabbit hole spiraling of fire trends in my home state.

The point was, River's Bend was now known because of a fire.

But before it had just been another small, quiet town on a river, known for our tight-knit community and our many, many festivals.

We loved an excuse for a celebration.

And we had many of them.

Including my favorite, the Wildflower Festival.

Just thinking that felt a bit like choosing my favorite child—*oh, no! You're ALL my favorite*—but the truth was that there was never a better time than April in Northern California. The hills were green, and the flowers were blooming, covering stretches of those green hills in bright swathes of color—Golden Poppies and Lupin and Wild Iris and Fireweed and more, so many different species.

So many colors.

So many signs of new life.

And I—for once—was dreading it, dreading celebrating that sign of new life and the bloom of spring. Because my heart was aching, that damned crevice in my chest was gaping, the walls within rattling, and I just...didn't want to be here.

I didn't want to be slapping on a smile and doing my job.

I wanted to be in my office at the apartment, playing with stickers.

I wanted to be cuddled with Joel, him healing the wounds inside me.

Except, he was married.

So, I was here, back aching after having slept in my office, not trusting the man to not circle back to the parking lot, to the hill-side under the dark, starry sky.

I didn't have a couch in my space at the newly rebuilt Civic Center, so I'd reclined in my chair.

And my back and neck and shoulders were hating me right then.

But I was still walking over to the flatbed truck parked just off of Main Street, ready to put my limited muscles to use and go about my orders.

Could I get out of those orders, considering I'd created the spreadsheet delegating tasks and then double-checked it that morning before I'd peeled my bare arms from the leather of my office chair? Yes.

Was I going to? No. I pulled my weight. Always.

And was I going to pretend I hadn't double checked to make sure everything was under control? Also, yes.

One of the only things my dad—a former mayor himself—had taught me about this job (in between berating me about my shortcomings), was that I definitely couldn't do it all myself. Which meant I needed our volunteers and paid staff to feel like I wasn't undercutting all of their hard work. So, I checked in at the volunteer table, I got my orders, and I got to work.

That was how we built a community where people worked together, where we had each other's backs and—

"Billie!"

I jerked, nearly running myself into a signpost—and seriously, what kind of city planner put a signpost *there*?

Grinning, knowing I was one of those city planners, I turned toward the voice.

Alex.

Bailey's stepson ran up to me, wrapping his arms around my middle and squeezing tight. Bailey, being my niece, who was two years younger than me, and more like a sister than anything else (but that was a story for another day) had stopped to talk to someone, but his mom, Veronica, was following, trailing behind her kiddo at a much more sedate pace.

Swear to God, I didn't want kids of my own.

But Axel—Bailey's man—and Veronica had made a gorgeous freaking kid.

Then again, Axel was pretty much the equivalent of a Greek God so...

Fill in the blanks for yourselves, kids.

Alex was adorable. And he was sweet.

And he had one of the biggest, kindest hearts I'd ever met.

In fact, he and Bailey could have a competition on that front, the latter having welcomed Alex and Veronica into hers and Axel's lives without the slightest bit of hesitation. But that wasn't for right now, not with my adorable stepnephew hugging me tight.

"Alex!" I exclaimed, cupping his cheek when he glanced up at me and smiled. "What are you guys doing here?"

A shrug, his arms dropping away. "Mom wanted some fresh air and Bailey said you can always use an extra pair of hands setting up for a festival."

"Well, Bailey doesn't lie," I said, ruffling his hair. "And I bet they'll need extra help at the"—I paused briefly, glanced up at Veronica, who'd come up more slowly behind Bailey and her kiddo, head covered by a purple knit beanie, face pale and a bit drawn, but looking much better than the last time I'd seen her, having finished with her cancer treatments for the moment—"hot chocolate stand," I finished after Veronica had answered my silent query communicated by eyebrow lift with a slight nod.

"Hot chocolate?" Alex's face lit up. "There's hot chocolate?"

I nodded, mouth curving. "There's always hot chocolate at festivals."

"I love River's Bend!" Alex shouted.

And I didn't bother to hide my grin.

Because me too. *Me* too.

"The stand is just the next block up," I said. "If you tell them Billie sent you, I bet they might even give you extra marshmallows once they're finished setting up."

"Whoa!" Alex said.

"We'll just go and see how we can help at the stand," Veronica said.

I leaned close as Alex skipped off toward the stand. "There's also a bench behind the stall," I murmured. "Just in case."

Veronica swallowed, her hand squeezing mine. "Thanks, Billie."

And then she was following Alex down the street, Bailey following them after a pitstop to give me a hug and tilting her head behind her, and saying, "The hockey muscle is here, by the way."

My stomach clenched. "I—"

But she was already turning away, walking after Veronica and Alex as my gaze shifted down the street, rotated toward where my niece had hitched her head.

I relaxed.

Fox—tall, bearded, tatted, and with a terrible sense of humor that called to the twelve-year-old boy inside her—was strolling down the street, big, bulky body loose and relaxed.

Ryan was beside him—smaller, leaner, and faster on the ice, with a soft heart and an ex-girlfriend who'd stomped on it.

Good guys.

Ones I could put to work and who wouldn't look too closely —okay, that wasn't true. They'd look closely, and they'd probably see too much and ask nosy questions. But Ry would back off when I made it clear I didn't want to talk (in fact, the only one he seemed incapable of giving distance to from was Veronica...who he babied until even V, the most patient person I'd ever met, lost her temper).

Fox would...well, the big brute didn't do anything he didn't want to.

But he could be distracted.

By that terrible twelve-year-old sense of humor.

Good. Plan. Distract the hockey muscle by putting them to work.

Go. *Break*. Clap hands or do...whatever they did on the football field.

Only just as I'd lifted my hand and waved, opening my mouth to flag them down, Fox shifted to the side...

And there was Joel.

His eyes came to mine and his stride hitched, just for a

moment. I watched his face change, his eyes narrow as they came to mine, throat working, hands fisting. Then he was moving toward me, determined and persistent and...

"Shit," I whispered, pulse hammering in my veins, my heart squeezing.

Fear and need and want and sadness and—

My emotions were all over the fucking place.

I backed up.

He kept coming.

My legs hit the cool metal of the truck.

He kept coming.

My hands pressed flat to the panel of the door, and I slid to the side, feeling the open tailgate dig into the backs of my thighs.

He. Kept. Coming.

Five feet between us. One. *There.*

I jerked, fingers brushing plants and plastic and dirt.

And I did the only thing I could.

I grabbed one of the plastic pots, lifted it...

And dumped it over his head.

SIX

JOEL

For a second, I'd been distracted by her.

How pretty she was without a lick of makeup on, her curls a riotous mess.

Then I noticed it wasn't only without a lick of makeup on, but it also appeared she was here without a lick of sleep the night before.

I knew the feeling.

Willow.

The divorce that wasn't a fucking divorce.

Christ.

At least now I could explain what had happened and what I was going to do.

I opened my mouth—

Soil rained down on my head, coating my face, my eyes and nose and lips and—*fuck*. My tongue. I was eating dirt.

Great.

But before I could do more than register that fact—and that my teammates had been witness to the pile of dirt being dumped over my head—Billie was pushing me back, was slipping from between me and the truck.

And...gone.

Hauling ass off Main Street, turning the corner toward City Hall.

Fox whistled. "Man, you must have really fucked up."

I didn't pay attention to him, or his shit-stirring, just turned and took off after Billie. And swear to fuck, I was getting tired of chasing her, tired of her running away, tired—

Of all this.

But I'd talked to Willow last night, and I had the story—or the story Willow was giving me, anyway. A lot of pieces were missing. She was holding back and being evasive. Bottom line? I needed to talk to a lawyer and get this shit sorted.

But I had enough details for the moment.

Enough to give the woman I loved an explanation.

Her curls bounced as she moved across the parking lot at the Civic Center, but I was taller and I had longer legs and I was gaining on her.

Had gained on her.

Had gotten close enough that I could snag her arm, drag her to a halt.

"Don't fucking touch me," she snapped.

"Tough shit," I snapped back. "I'm already touching you."

She glared at me over her shoulder. "How juvenile of you."

"Sort of like"—I waved my free hand at myself, hair to shoulders, feeling the dirt coating me scattering as I moved, like fucked-up glitter being sprinkled onto a craft project—"throwing dirt on someone."

"I didn't throw dirt."

I lifted a brow.

Her cheeks went pink. "I didn't."

I held her eyes, lifted the other one.

"I just...*dumped* it."

That had me snorting, my hand flexing as I turned her to face me, getting dirt in her hair, on her clothes.

Seemed fair enough to me.

"That's what you're going with, sweetheart?" I asked, dancing the fingers of my free hand over her cheek, leaving a smear of soil behind.

"It's what you deserve." She gripped my hand, pulled it from her arm, and stepped back, breaking contact.

"Why's that?"

Now *her* brows came up. "You're seriously asking me that question?" She thumped a hand to her chest. "Me, your girlfriend, who opened the door to the apartment I'd just moved into to see *Willow*, your *wife*—"

"She's not my wife."

Her brows curved further, into tiny sideways Cs on her forehead.

"Okay," I said, rubbing my forehead. "Willow is my wife."

She flinched, took another step back.

I lifted my hands, palms out. "Technically."

Another flinch. More distance between us.

"I thought I divorced her, sweetheart."

A scoff. "How can you think you divorced someone?"

Yeah, there it was. The crux of this situation, and the focal point of my stupidity. "I filled out the paperwork, gave it to my attorney, and I"—a shake of my head, my hand coming up to rub the ache from my temples—"was traded and heartbroken and...I didn't follow up."

"You're kidding me, right?" Billie snapped.

I wished I was.

I wished I could say this was a dumb misunderstanding and not—

"You're still married because you didn't *follow up?*"

She chuckled, but it wasn't amused, wasn't warm and bright like her normal giggles, nor like the belly laughs that filled the space with her big, buoyant presence, that got everyone else laughing, even though she was hurting inside and hiding.

From everyone but me.

Which was why I kept pushing, kept fighting for her. "Just let me explain—"

"You didn't *follow up*." A shake of her head as she turned away. "Fuck. I can't with this. I can't"—a wave of her hand—"do this shit today."

Fuck. Still running.

And I was still chasing.

And I was still...tired.

She started away from me again, and I ground my teeth together, taking a long, slow breath, mind reeling, trying to find some way to explain this so we could put it behind us. Some explanation that would be enough.

Some way *I* would be enough.

But...all I did was clench my teeth together and stand there, watching her walk away.

Exhausted.

"Rosie." My voice broke as her name burst out of me, rasping and almost intelligible.

But I knew she heard it, even though her back was still to me, because she froze. Then her neck twisted, and her eyes came to mine and—

"Don't walk away from me," I pleaded.

Her eyes widened. "Joel."

"Please," I whispered. "Just don't walk away...not this time."

She stilled again, lips moving, but no sound reaching my ears. Then her feet moved, and she turned to face me, expression stark.

"I didn't follow up," I blurted. "I'm not saying it was smart or even close to it. But it was five years ago. I thought that chapter of my life was closed." I shoved a hand through my hair, scattering dirt everywhere. "We got married quickly—too quickly—too soon after starting dating to know that we weren't compatible. And... it wasn't working."

Billie's eyes softened, giving me a glimpse of that gentle soul and soft heart as she moved back toward me. "Why?"

"What?"

"Why wasn't it working?"

"It just..." I shook my head. "Wasn't. Mostly because of stupid things, really. Stuff that we would have figured out if we'd been dating longer and I wasn't on the road half the time. She liked to stay in. I wanted to go out, to do all the things I didn't get to do when I was working. She didn't like Indian food and—" I broke off, knowing I was prattling.

"It's your favorite." A beat. "What else?"

"She was obsessive about separating the darks and lights, would flip out if a sock even touched her white towels. And if I snored, or left beard hairs on the counter, or didn't roll the toothpaste tube right. And I was just as bad—her makeup on the counter drove me nuts and the way she chewed her chips. Fuck, she put milk in the bowl *before* her cereal." I shook my head. "Small shit. All of it dumb as fuck."

"But not to you then." A beat. "Not to either of you."

"No," I agreed. "Back then, it seemed big, *too* big. Insurmountable to the point that we needed to separate and..." I sighed. "She said she wanted to be done. So." A shrug. "I let her go."

Silence, Billie's brows dragging together. "You let her go."

"I mean," I whispered. "She didn't want to be married to me. Not really. So"—I shrugged—"what else could I do?"

"You didn't fight for her."

I hadn't. "No, Rosie, I didn't."

She rocked back on her heels. "But..."

She was closer now, close enough I could smell the soft floral scent of her shampoo, her lotion. Close enough that my fingers could brush her skin if I allowed myself.

"But," she said again, "you're fighting for me."

My inhale was sharp.

"You're here, chasing after me, fighting for me even though I dumped soil on your head and pushed you away again and—" Her breathing hitched, and she pressed a hand to her mouth.

"Shit, honey," she whispered. "I am so fucked up."

SEVEN

BILLIE ROSE

Guilt was a torrent inside me, building and spinning and twisting my insides.

I wanted to run.

I wanted to seize this moment and declare, "See?! I told you! He couldn't love me! He's a liar, and he doesn't love me!"

Except, he'd gotten divorced over a toothpaste tube.

And I'd just dumped a pot of soil over his head, and he'd chased me, was fighting for me, after he'd fought for me in front of my parents, had fought to get through my walls.

Fought for me.

Me.

"I am so fucked up," I whispered.

His face changed and then he was there, arms around me, warmth surrounding me, one of his hands on the back of my head, the other at my hip, drawing me against him. "No, you're not," he whispered.

"I am," I said, melting against him, my forehead resting on his chest. I could feel the dirt on my skin, clinging to the cotton of his Rush T-shirt. "I am *so* totally fucked up."

"You're—"

I lifted my head, rose on tiptoe to cup his jaw. "And I'm sorry. Really. I am."

He exhaled. "I didn't know. I promise, I didn't know that—"

My eyes slid closed, and I leaned closer, nuzzled his throat.

Dirt in my mouth for my trouble.

Well deserved.

"I'm sorry," I said again.

His arms tightened. "Hush, now. It's okay, Rosie baby."

Rosie baby.

That warmed my belly, and...made me feel even worse. "I'm—"

His palm came to my jaw, cupping it, drawing my face away from him, holding my head in place so that our gazes connected, so I couldn't look away, couldn't break that contact without closing my eyes.

And I didn't want to do that.

Because he was so beautiful, and I loved him and—

This was all so stupid. *I* was stupid and—

Enough.

I needed to channel my inner Billie Rose—the Billie Rose that was the kickass mayor of River's Bend who got shit done and didn't wither when things got hard, not the Billie Rose I'd been since the moment I'd opened that door to see Willow on the doorstep.

Not the Billie Rose who was looking for, anticipating, *expecting* the moment when everything would go wrong.

And seizing it.

Because that was less scary than...what I was feeling in my heart, my mind, my—

Fingers gently brushing my skin. "Can we talk about the rest of it?" he teased gently. "Or do you need more time to spiral?"

I'd gone stiff at the first question. The second made me jerk against his hold, glare up at him. "Hilarious," I muttered.

"I know," he said softly, dropping his hand from my jaw and lacing our fingers together, drawing me forward.

Toward the newly rebuilt Civic Center and City Hall.

"It's closed," I murmured.

He glanced down at me, mouth curved. "Well, funny story, I happen to know a woman with a key."

That was true.

Somewhat annoyingly so.

But I'd already picked an unnecessary fight in the last twelve hours. I should probably cool it.

Leading the way to the double doors, I tugged at my keycard—attached to a spoolie at my hip—lifting it to the scanner at the side entrance, hearing the lock *click* as it disengaged, the light on the gray plastic pad flashing green for a moment.

Joel reached past me and tugged at the handle, holding it open for me to precede him.

I led the way down the hall and up through the stairwell then through another hall and into my office.

To my desk.

Sitting in my chair with a wince.

Expecting Joel to follow, to stand between my legs and my desk, his big body blocking my computer screen like usual.

Instead, he had paused in my doorway with narrowed eyes.

"What?" I asked, starting to stand.

He moved then, assuming his typical position, our knees bumping together, our bodies close. The scowl on his face was easily discernible.

"What?" I repeated.

"You slept here last night."

Not a question.

I winced. "Um..."

"You don't even have a couch here, Rosie baby," he grumbled. "Where'd you sleep? That chair?"

I winced again.

He sighed, shook his head. "What am I going to do with you, huh?"

Love me?

I almost asked it—in fact, the question had bubbled up in the back of my throat, had actually danced along my tongue, threatened to escape through my lips just before I caught it at the tip and bit it back.

"Where I slept doesn't matter," I said, adding when his scowl deepened, "because you need to tell me all that you found out about this situation with Willow," I said instead of blurting out my guts...or worse, my *feelings*. "And then I'm going to put on my mayoral problem-solving hat, and we're going to sort our shit out."

He sighed, leaned back against my desk, then bent and hooked a hand between my legs—something that made me gasp, even though he wasn't cupping me *between* my legs. He'd gripped the bottom of my chair to roll it closer, and I felt that movement in my pussy, in the slightly rough show of strength.

I felt it *everywhere*.

Thank fuck we'd made up.

Because our knees were touching again, and I wanted...

"Rosie baby," he murmured, lightly tugging at a curl.

God, I loved it when he did that—loved when he was close, loved it when he made it clear he liked to be near me, loved it when he...did pretty much anything.

Focus.

"Tell me about the divorce—or lack thereof, anyway."

He grimaced. "It was five years ago—supposed to be finalized five years ago, that is. We'd started the divorce before that, but we weren't rushing because she didn't have her green card yet."

I frowned. "Is that why you guys got married so fast?"

A shrug. "It was either get married or Willow had to go home.

Her extra year was up—she was an au pair, and already had one extension—and we were in the fuck-like-rabbits stage so neither one of us wanted to be apart—" He broke off, probably because I'd made a sound like a dying animal. "Sorry, sweetheart." He brushed my cheek lightly. "I just mean we were attached, and when she tried for another extension, they denied it."

"Attached," I said softly.

"Yeah," he said just as softly.

"And she married you so she could stay."

He nodded and exhaled. "You're not wrong." His gaze went distant. "The option was her leaving, or us getting married. Obviously, we chose door number two."

"Yeah."

His eyes slid away, a muscle in his cheek flexing, his lips pressed flat.

I hated that—the stress, the sadness, the confusion, the way his past was dragging him a million miles away from me.

I wanted to lighten the mood, was almost desperate to do it.

My fingers found his leg, squeezed lightly. "Is this the point where I should inform you that it's stupid to tell a public official you've committed a crime?"

Those green eyes went wide, head swiveling back.

My lips curved. "Yup," I said. "I could turn you in to the authorities." I tapped my fingers together, evil genius style. "Just think of all the blackmail material you just gave me."

"Funny," he muttered, leaning in and pushing back an unruly curl.

Then pausing, holding it between thumb and forefinger, rubbing the strands gently, back and forth, back and forth.

"She told my attorney that we changed our minds." A shake of his head. "I'd done my part, got the shit signed." His hand slid down and he cupped my jaw. "But with the trade—it came through right as everything was imploding—and then the one not long after that—the one that brought me here—I didn't realize that I'd never received the final paperwork. I just...signed and dropped them off and figured that chapter of my life was closed."

Only it wasn't.

And five years later...

"So, why did she change her mind?"

Also, why hadn't his attorney double-checked with him? At a minimum, that seemed like negligence to just now follow up. Right?

A sigh. "She wouldn't tell me." His laugh was disbelieving. "She was sitting on the stairs when I got back last night and admitted that she'd gone around my back to delay the divorce, but when I asked her *why* the fuck she would do that, she just...shut down." A shake of his head. "Just told me she'd fix it and to be patient, and then she left."

"She told *you* to be patient?" I asked.

A nod.

"After she lied to you and your attorney?"

Another incline of his head.

"After five years?"

"Yup."

"And showing up like she did?"

"Yeah, sweetheart."

"What a bitch," I muttered.

"I'm not disagreeing with you." He exhaled, shook his head. "I need to make an appointment with a lawyer here in town. I don't trust her."

I snorted. No shit.

"I just...I can't believe she would do that." He clicked his tongue. "The Willow I knew would never have done anything like this."

Then again, they apparently hadn't known each other all that long, had they?

I didn't say that, though, didn't pour salt on the wound. I just settled my hand on his knee, squeezed lightly, and stayed close.

He'd had a shock, and I hadn't made it better. The least I could do was be here with him, to be supportive in this moment. But as the quiet continued, I found a different question slipping from my tongue, sliding free before I comprehended it was trying to sneak out, to pollute the moment of peace we'd settled in to. "Did you love her?"

"I—" He exhaled, shook his head. "I *thought* I did."

That stung, no joke, but thankfully Joel kept talking, distracting me from the fact that this man had been so infatuated —maybe so in love—with Willow that he'd married her so they didn't have to be apart.

"But what I felt for her isn't even a fraction of what I feel for you."

EIGHT

JOEL

She wasn't running.

She'd frozen, plump lips parting on a surprised exhale.

I tugged at her chair, drew her even closer, until our legs were slotted together like two puzzle pieces.

Perfect fit.

"Joel," she whispered.

"I know," I whispered back.

"The feelings I have for you—" Her words dissolved in a croak. "I-I—"

"It's okay, Rosie baby."

"It's not. I"—a breath, deep and heavy and long—"I'm sorry," she said, meeting my eyes, rising out of her chair, body leaning close to mine. No, leaning *against* mine. All those curves. All that lush woman.

The chair slid back, and her hands were on my shoulders, some of her weight on my thigh where it remained woven through hers, the rest was in her hands on my body, her breasts pushing against my chest, her belly pressing to mine.

Not an inch between us.

Just as I liked.

Our mouths were close too, breaths mingling, her eyes near enough that I could see the flecks of gold and gray among that sea of sky blue.

"I'm sorry," she said again.

"You don't have to—"

Even closer, her lips brushing mine as she spoke. "I do. I'm sorry. I'll do better. *Be* better."

"Rosie baby," I began. "That's not what I want." I didn't want her to change. Not really. I just...wanted more of that good we had —the smiles she gave me when she looked up from her work and saw me there, her warm body lax against mine when she slept, her eyes gentle and her words soft and that slice of vulnerable she gave me, and *only* me.

"I know," she murmured. "I know." A sigh. "But for me, for us, I...need to do better, yeah?"

"Yeah, sweetheart." I lifted a hand, weaved it through her curls. "And for my part, I'll try not to have any other ex-wives pop out of the woodwork, okay?"

A chuckle, not quite as light and sparkling as normal, and not her big belly laughs that filled rooms with warmth.

But it was something.

As was...*this.*

Talking. Working shit out.

My mouth curved. "Look at us."

One brow lifted.

A nod down at our bodies. "Being adults and shit."

She glanced down, face softening, eyes darkening to navy, lips parting, and just the barest hint of pink dancing to life on her cheeks. "Ah."

I tugged at a curl, watching it straighten then bounce back to a perfect spiral. "What?"

That pink spread, and I felt a growing warmth in my stomach, arrowing south, like teasing fingers drifting along my cock. Then those phantom fingers were gripping tight, stroking hard as wicked danced with the gold flecks and deep blue of her irises, mischief gentling her expression and melting her body against mine.

"I was thinking you were talking about how good our bodies look pressed together."

My dick twitched. "Tease."

A brush of her mouth over mine. "You like it." A beat. "*And* our bodies pressed together."

"True. Though"—I gripped her bottom lip between my teeth, tugged lightly—"I have to say that I like it when our bodies are naked and pressed together more."

She stilled, leaning back slightly, studying my eyes.

I was studying her back, my nerves prickling, fingers tingling.

Naughty. She looked fucking *naughty*.

My dick twitched again—hell, who was I kidding? My dick was hard, and it was slowly losing interest in the conversation. It wanted to explore that wicked and naughty, not rehash the past, not think about Willow and the fucked-up situation she'd dropped at my door.

"Hmm," she said softly, hand sliding up from my shoulder, along my neck, to my jaw, nails sliding lightly through my beard.

Goose bumps.

The woman always gave me goose bumps when her hands were on me, when her fingertips trailed over my skin, when her nails bit lightly into my flesh.

Or harder.

Sometimes I liked harder.

And...speaking of harder—

My eyes flicked down.

Billie's did too, and then her mouth tipped up, naughtiness expanding. I reached for her hips, starting to draw her even nearer, wanting to drag that pussy up and down my thigh, to encourage her to grind against me until—

She hopped off my lap.

No. *No.*

Not that.

"*Rosie,*" I rasped.

The chair sailed back even further, crashing into the wall. Okay. I liked *that.* More room. More space to do the things I wanted to do to her.

But she didn't come back to me, just circumvented the desk and moved to the door.

"I—"

Click.

My neck twisted, gaze going over my shoulder, seeing Billie turning away from the heavy wooden panel, the lock now engaged.

My dick didn't just twitch this time. It went rock-hard.

But...this was her office and her work and—

She came back over to me, hand on my jaw, cupping it for a moment before it slid down my throat, paused to press lightly on my chest, over my heart. "Big feelings," she whispered, sending the organ thumping against my rib cage, pounding harder, pulse thundering through my veins. "*Huge.*"

I sucked in a breath then released it in a hiss. "Rosie baby."

A smile before that hand began moving again, sliding lower, over my pecs, along my stomach, to the waistband of my jeans.

"*Rosie,*" I rasped as her palm cupped what was now the rock-hard length of my cock through my jeans.

That smile widened.

And she dropped to her knees.

I inhaled so rapidly that I almost choked on my own saliva, but then Billie was moving, her fingers working at the button on my jeans, tugging at the zipper, drawing it down, parting the material, shoving at it until my dick popped free, springing toward her face like it was a sentient being and knew that it wanted to be sliding between those pale pink lips.

She leaned in, flicking her tongue over the head of my cock.

I cursed again, legs threatening to buckle, thighs shaking, knees knocking. All that conditioning on and off the ice didn't make one bit of a difference, not with my Rosie girl's mouth on me.

Her lips parted, and her fingers wrapped around the base of my cock, and then—

"*Fuck*," I growled.

Slick. No. *Wet.* Tight. Hot.

Her tongue circled the head of my dick, lingering on the sensitive spot near the tip, making me shudder, my hands diving into her hair, wanting to thrust deep.

Desperate to fuck that mouth.

Long lashes.

She stared up at me through long, long lashes, my cock still in her mouth, her words slightly muffled. "Do it."

My fingers tightened in her hair.

My dick hardened further, grew bigger.

A slow stroke of that tongue. A firm grip clenching tighter.

Suction.

"Do it," she murmured, dragging her tongue up the shaft, fist working, lips hovering at the top of my cock.

Then she parted her lips, slid deep, so deep that it felt like I'd gone well beyond bumping into the back of her throat, that I was down her throat, swallowed and—

"*Fuck,*" I hissed, hips jerking.

She moaned.

My head dropped back, eyes slamming closed, shutting out the fluorescent lights overhead, the world, shutting out everything except that tight, wet mouth around my cock.

A long, slow glide of her sliding free, tongue working, hand tight.

"Fuck my mouth, honey."

Honey.

Fuck, I loved when she called me *honey*.

Lips parting, she sucked me deep again, tempting and slow and driving me insane inch by inch.

Then her hand was working at my jeans again and they were sliding lower, halfway down my thighs.

A warm palm snaked between them, slid up, cupped my balls.

I cursed again, hips jerking, and then the woman did something absolutely illegal with her tongue.

And I lost control.

NINE

BILLIE ROSE

I knew the exact moment that he lost his fight at control.

Mostly because his dick swelled even further, stretching at the sides of my mouth, making the corners burn.

I wanted him inside me.

To feel that same stretch and burn between my legs.

But I wanted this first—him hard and deep, thrusting until it felt like I couldn't breathe, his fingers tangled in my hair, biting into my scalp.

"Fuck," he growled, and I didn't know why that sent a shiver down my spine, had desire pooling in my belly, drenching my pussy, but when his voice went all raspy and growly and—

Another sign of losing control.

Another way this big, strong hockey player was mine.

Mine.

Then he was moving, fucking my mouth like I'd asked, like I'd demanded, cock gliding into my throat, pressing deep until my eyes watered, tears clinging to my lashes, until I had to swallow down a cough.

Swallow *him* down.

"Fuck," he growled again, clearly feeling that, clearly *liking* that, pumping harder and faster, sending desire swirling through my belly, sharp empty pangs of need into my pussy.

So I did it again.

Reveled in his curses and his reaction and the fact that he was close.

I massaged his balls, sucked him hard, gripped him tight...and felt like I was the one who was going to come.

I moaned—

He pulled out, the long, thick length of his cock glistening under the overhead lights of my office. It was red and swollen, almost angry, and I wanted it deep again, wanted it almost choking me again.

But Joel was moving, moving so quickly that I could barely process the motion.

Then I felt it.

His hands on my clothes, yanking my shirt over my head, my bra joining it in fluttering to the ground barely a heartbeat later. The button on my jeans was torn open, my pants and underwear shoved down to my thighs.

My ass hit the edge of my desk and I had to hold on tight so I didn't slide off as he wrenched at the material of my jeans, jerking it down my legs, pausing only to rip off my shoes and toss them aside.

Naked.

Except for my socks.

Joel yanked off his shirt, tossed it aside, but he didn't do anything further with his jeans, the material straining at the power of his muscular thighs, hard cock bobbing slightly as he moved back toward me.

Lifted me.

I gasped, clung to his forearms.

But then he was setting me back down onto my feet, only this time I was facing away from him. One big, warm hand pressed between my shoulder blades, encouraging me down onto the surface of the desk. Papers scattered, pens and paper clips dug into my skin. My keyboard protested as my front hit the keys, making a soft, angry beeping sound as it tried to communicate with my sleeping computer.

His hand slid down, along the bumps of my spine, stopping just at the top of my ass, a finger dipping into the cleft between my cheeks.

Stroking.

Making me want him there.

"This ass," he groaned.

I arched, thighs parting, ass tipped up. Trying to tempt him. Trying to—

Crack!

A sharp smack over one cheek.

"Behave," he muttered, sliding that finger lower, sweeping it through the wet heat between my legs, dipping that finger inside.

I gasped, his name on my tongue, in the air.

Another finger, those blunt digits spreading wide, stretching me. Then pulling out and thrusting back in.

Hard. Rough.

Just like I needed it.

But not enough.

Something he knew—because of course he did. Joel knew me, every inch and thought and worry. He slipped a third finger in and now his name on my tongue was more scream than gasp, my body lost in a whirlwind of pleasure even as my mind had paused, stopped to consider if I knew him as well as he did me.

He'd been married before.

And I hadn't known.

Been traded, several times at least, between teams I didn't know.

I'd met his family once, and I'd been late, a total mess that he'd needed to talk back from the edge.

He knew I didn't like beer, knew the brand wine I preferred, had tracked me down even though a crisis had landed on his porch. I'd launched his gifts to me over a cliff, gifts that were thoughtful and sweet and proved that he knew every part of me—

And I needed to do better.

Because, worst of all, I'd hurt him.

But before I could tell him that, make the promise in my mind out loud, make it real and make sure he knew I understood, his fingers slid out of me, leaving me empty and bereft and—

His big body bending over mine, mouth coming to my ear, teeth capturing the lobe for one sharp nip. "Behave." Another *crack* that had my ass stinging, had my skin heating, had my pussy growing even more wet.

"I'm...not...even...moving," I protested, the words puffed out through my heaving lungs, my voice like sandpaper.

"But your mind is." Another nip. "Stay here with me, Rosie baby. Stay here and be *with me.*"

I'd hurt him, and I'd let him carry more than his fair share of weight in this relationship far too often. I could push my thoughts away, stow that promise I needed to make for a later date. I could be here with him—at the very least I could do *that.*

I arched against him, one hand lifting, diving into his hair. "Okay, honey."

He straightened, dislodging my hold, his palm skating over my ass, and I braced, waiting for the smack, more than a little desperate for it. But instead, it slid up again, along my back, caressing my sides, dipping down to stroke along the sides of my breasts.

Kneading lightly at one shoulder than the other.

Gripping my throat, turning my head so that I could see him— could see *him* behind me. So I couldn't see anything *except* him. And it was a beautiful sight. My man. My hockey player. Huge, his muscles standing out in stark relief, emerald eyes darkened so they looked almost black and the heat, the need that poured out of them, threatened to reduce me to ash.

He kicked my legs apart, came closer.

His other hand went to my hip, gripping tight.

"Hold on, baby."

An order.

One I barely had the chance to process, let alone follow through on—and what was there to hold on to, anyway?

Paperclips?

Pens?

My keyboard?

I didn't get the chance to try because his cock was sliding through my wet pussy, notching at my entrance, and pushing in.

Stretching.

Burning.

Good.

"Joel," I moaned.

"This fucking cunt," he growled, fingers tightening on my throat, gripping my hip. "Drives me fucking insane."

"I was—" A gasp because he started moving.

"Hush," he muttered, thrusting in, pelvis flush to my ass, balls smacking against the tops of my thighs.

"I was going—"

"*Hush.*" A stroke in. Deep, hard, *good.*

"To say—"

Teeth pressing into my skin, his hips pistoning faster now. "Hush, sweetheart."

My brain was short-circuiting, trying futilely to hold on to words, to finish my thought. "To say..." Joel was pounding into me, each thrust somehow harder than the last, and it was hell on my concentration, on my ability to speak any sort of sense.

His hand slid into my hair and wound his fingers into the strands, jerked my head back, making my scalp sting. But it wasn't too much. With Joel, it was *never* too much. It was the perfect mix of pleasure and pain, of yearning and sensation. "I *said* hush, sweetheart."

"Okay," I whispered.

"Unless you're moaning my name," he said, and I heard the laughter in his tone as he came close, those teeth on my earlobe again, his voice hot in my ear. "Then you can say whatever the fuck you want to say."

My head was spinning.

My pussy was aching.

My body was tense and trembling.

I couldn't say anything besides his name, and even then, it was a moan, a rasp, a...scream as pleasure spiraled tighter and tighter, a spring winding inside me, twisting, spinning, growing more and more tense.

And then that tension sprang, and the spring uncoiled and—

I flew, pleasure splintering through me.

The last thing I heard was Joel shouting *my* name.

TEN

JOEL

"Your shirt's on backwards," Fox said, my annoying ass teammate coming up behind me and shoving at my shoulder.

I'd just had an orgasm that had nearly torn me in half, so I didn't give in to the urge to punch the fucker in the face, but I did stick my foot out, sending him tripping as he tried to step up onto the sidewalk, a bag of soil hefted on each shoulder.

Ha.

Fucker.

I stepped carefully onto the curb, carrying my own load to the tables that were set up for kids to repot some native wildflowers.

Some would be planted in a few weeks in the local parks and at school gardens, but today, those baby wildflowers would be transplanted by teen and adult volunteers all along Main Street into a bevy of huge terra-cotta pots someone had donated to the city, brightening the sidewalk and "bringing joy" (the latter being Billie's perspective when she'd returned to the apartment, skipping with happiness at her luck a few weeks back).

Later that afternoon, the townspeople would disperse into the hillsides, each with their own seed packets—purchased or won from the game booths or given away if the kids completed the scavenger hunt. Volunteers would guide them, or they could venture out along their favorite trails, scattering seeds in the state and regional preserves, hopefully extending the bloom in the fire-rich soil.

More native plants.

More pretty flowers.

Less brown.

That was my summary of Billie's excitement for her "favorite" festival. I liked to tease her that every festival was her favorite, but I knew that she'd told me the truth. I'd seen it in every minute of preparation and the way her face had lit up during the planning process.

My woman loved a plan.

But this event was next level.

I placed my bags near the table where Billie was setting out a bevy of small, compostable pots and buckets of soil and shovels.

She had a dusting of soil in her hair, a smear of dirt on one cheek.

I thought her hair was my fault—transferred from me to her— knew the cheek definitely was. The streaks on her shirt probably came from her filling up the buckets.

Or maybe me.

I was fine with either.

Fox stepped up next to me, grunting as he let his bags drop to the ground. "Let's see," he drawled, tapping his finger to his chin. "The woman has a coy smile and Just Been Fucked hair." He clapped me on the shoulder. "I see you've taken a page out of the Fox Brown playbook of conflict resolution."

"I don't know what you're talking about," I muttered, watching as Billie crouched slightly so a teenage boy could whisper in her ear.

She nodded, glanced over at me, and smiled, lifting a finger, telling me silently to wait a minute.

"Billie!" Fox shouted, making the teenage boy jump.

She shifted her focus to Fox, lifted a brow, and called, "Yes?"

"Julian, there, has the best slap shot I've ever seen for a kid his age."

Julian went still, his arms and legs seeming too long for his frame. Lanky and tall and awkward, but Fox was right. I'd seen Julian on the ice more than a few times—early mornings, late nights, practicing every chance he got.

And he put those lanky limbs to work with a wicked snapper and a long ass stride that allowed him haul ass on the ice.

"I saw him play last month," Billie called back, ruffling Julian's hair. "He's gonna be better than you in no time."

Julian's cheeks went pink, and he ducked his head.

"Damn right, he is!" Fox called back.

Okay, now those cheeks had gone straight from pink to fire engine red.

Billie winked then ruffled Julian's hair again, said something that I couldn't hear, but that something didn't have the red abating in the least. Then Julian was loping off and Billie was coming our way, those lush curves no less tempting even though I'd had them not an hour before.

"Your shirt's on backwards," she said, mouth tipped up at the edges as she came near.

Fox busted up.

I narrowed my eyes at both of them, but yanked at my shirt sleeves, pulling one arm in and tugging the material around so it was on correctly.

In fairness, I hadn't much wanted to get dressed, not after the orgasm that had nearly killed me.

Ryan made it to the table as Fox's laughter continued to ring through the air. He paused, brows pulled together as he dropped the bags of soil he'd been carrying onto the ground, and asked, "What's so funny?"

"Madam Mayor is." Fox winked at my woman, and I knew he did it just to piss me off, the same reason he added, "No slippers today, princess?"

Swear to fuck. This man and his foot fetish.

Billie lifted a leg, showing off a foot clad in plain gray sneakers streaked with dirt. "I have my big girl shoes on today."

Waggling brows, a seductive tone that raised my hackles when Fox said, "I can give *you* something big."

And swear to fuck, if I didn't love the man, value him as a teammate and a friend, as someone who'd taken my back repeatedly on and off the ice, I would want to murder him.

Okay, fine. I *still* wanted to murder him.

Just for looking at my Rosie.

Definitely for flirting with her.

Billie, though—as always when dealing with Fox's shenanigans—was amused. "Yeah, you'd give me something big." Her lips tipped up. "A big ol' dose of disappointment."

Ryan choked.

I grinned.

Fox, as usual, was unaffected by the burn. He just leaned in, reached for a curl—

"Don't," I growled.

Fox's eyes cut to mine, and he deliberately tugged at the strand of hair.

"I'm going to kill you," I muttered.

Billie batted his hand away then leaned over the table and pressed her mouth to mine. "If you kill him, then that means you have to carry more bags of soil," she said, pulling back slightly, running her fingers through my beard, calming me even though her eyes were dancing with mischief. "And," she went on, "just for his nonsense, I'll put him on face-painting duty."

Fox had been chortling next to me, enjoying the burn.

Billie's words had him freezing.

"You wouldn't," he muttered.

"Dessie!" Billie called in answer, waving at her friend. "I've got a *big*"—she smirked at Fox—"canvas for you and the kids to practice on."

Dessie, never one to miss an opportunity to dish it back at Fox (read: torture him), grinned widely and hopped right on board with Billie's plan, twisting the screws in a way that I knew Fox wouldn't be able to weasel out:

Getting kids involved.

The man had a soft spot for kids.

"What do you think, guys?" Dessie asked the group of kids who were helping at the booth, all of whom looked to be between eight and ten years old. "What kind of face paint should Mr. Fox get?"

"A bumblebee!" one shouted.

"Stingers. Cool colors." Fox shrugged. "I can deal with that."

"Spiderman!" one of the boys called.

"Okay," Fox muttered. "That's better."

"A princess!" from behind them.

From *Billie*.

I glanced at her, brows raised.

She shrugged, fighting a smile. "Seems fitting."

"Sold!" Dessie called, picking up a palette of face paint and a brush. "Let's make Mr. Fox a princess, everyone!"

The boys scowled, but the girls screamed—and there were more of them, so they were louder, drowning out any protests as they swarmed out from behind the booth, grabbed Fox's hands, and hauled him forward.

"A purple princess!" one said, dancing as they dragged him along.

"With glitter!" said another, excitement in her little body.

"And lots and *lots* of pink!"

"And flowers!" from behind them. Again.

Fox groaned.

But to his credit, he just let the girls drag him along, draw him forward to the face-painting booth and shove him down into a chair.

Kids. Fox. Kryptonite.

I needed to remember that—solely for research purposes.

I glanced at Billie, genuinely confused. "How the hell do you use face paint to make someone a princess?"

She shrugged, mirth in her pretty blue eyes. "Beats me." She giggled, eyes flicking toward Fox, whose face was already covered in a shocking amount of pink and purple and glitter and flowers, given how little time had passed. "But I know those girls are going to do their best to make it happen."

ELEVEN

BILLIE ROSE

I was going to stop answering the door.

I really was.

But, in fairness, it was Game Night, and I was expecting company...I just wasn't expecting it to be of the willowy blonde variety.

Of the *Willow* variety.

Joel's not-so-ex was standing on the welcome mat I'd just bought from the home goods store downtown—Holly's Homey Goods—feet on the pretty floral design and I knew it was jealousy and insecurity that had me wanting to tell her to step back, to not dirty the rug...that people were supposed to wipe their feet on.

I didn't, though.

And look at me, identifying my feelings but not acting on them—albeit not at this moment. Who knew when I might snap and take this straight to a knockdown, drag-out catfight in the center of River's Bend.

"Willow," I said, not stepping out of the opening, but my voice was neutral (and look at me go again!). "Joel isn't here."

"I know."

That had my brows lifting. Okaaay.

Her expression changed, a glimpse of something I couldn't read drifting across her face so quickly I couldn't discern it. I only knew that it had a blip of cold sliding down my spine, one that didn't completely disappear when Willow shrugged, smiled a smile that was model beautiful, and said, "I heard the team was practicing while dining at one of the delightful restaurants downtown."

Delightful? What, was she a wannabe duchess? Or one of those WASP-y women who always wore a scarf in a convertible and called everyone *Darling?*

Because they were weirdly formal words.

Nice on the surface, but an undercurrent of something else beneath. And frankly, I didn't think anyone would call one of the restaurants in downtown River's Bend delightful—not even the owners.

Fresh, farm-to-table.

Delicious but informal.

Good service, big portions, nothing frozen unless it was bar food at Monroe's because fried *everything* made up the majority of the menu—as was necessary to pair correctly with the beers on draft. Dessie, who'd recently taken over management, was changing that slowly by incorporating fresh ingredients and new dishes, but if someone wanted mozzarella sticks or fish and chips or potato skins that were fried, loaded with cheese and green onions, bacon and sour cream, Monroe's was where they went.

Where they expected those dishes to be on offer.

What fried mozzarella sticks *weren't*, even amongst the laxest of critics?

Delightful.

So, there was something off about Willow's tone, something stranger than the odd formality. It was...a thread of derision, I thought, sitting just beneath those words. Or maybe I was assuming too much, was protective of my town and people and reading too much into it all? Maybe she was just insecure and shy?

Something that was supported when Willow nibbled on the corner of her mouth then glanced up at me through long, thick, perfectly curled lashes, "I actually came by to apologize."

Great. Now I felt like a dick.

Because my protective hackles had gone up and...because I didn't want to hear an apology from a beautiful, well-dressed woman who'd slept with Joel, who'd been married to him, who'd deceived him, and who'd—

Willow shifted from foot to foot.

My throat went tight, and it took a lot of effort to clear it, to be in this moment, to force out the words, "For what?"

Eyes shifting to the side then back to mine. "Could we...um... talk inside?"

Another bead of cold, another twist of my insides. But I didn't really have any reason *not* to let her inside. Plus, if I got her comfortable, gave her a glass of wine, I might loosen her up enough to get the full story, to get some details that would help Joel understand what had gone down.

Something other than saying she'd changed her mind.

So, I pushed away my discomfort, plastered on my media-ready smile, and stepped back. "Of course," I told her. "Why don't you have a seat in the family room?" I waved a hand toward my couch, in the direction of my kickass throw pillows I'd also bought downtown, and asked, "Can I get you a cup of coffee? Or would you rather have a glass of wine?"

"No, no," Willow said, perching on the couch like it was going to open up and eat her. "I don't want to be any trouble."

She didn't want to be trouble.

More than the whole changing-her-mind-five-years-ago variety?

More than the showing up and introducing herself as Joel's

wife when she hadn't seen or spoken to him in those years and couldn't have known who I was when I'd answered the door?

(But *should* have assumed I was someone important).

More than—

Breathe. I turned for the kitchen while I did that and when I'd calmed I spoke again. "Oh no," I told her breezily, not allowing my mind to be swept along. "You're not any trouble." I waited a beat, waited as that sat in the air, sank into the conversation— and hopefully into Willow's mind—then asked, "Red or white?"

Willow didn't reply for a long moment then said softly, "White."

I grinned at her over my shoulder. "That's my favorite."

Then I was in the kitchen and moving to the cabinet that held our wine glasses, tugging two down, channeling my mayoral powers by calling, "You hungry?"

"Oh no, I'm fine. I don't want to be any troub..."

I popped my head through the opening, smiling at her, waiting a moment as she trailed off before telling her again, "You're not any trouble."

(And vowing to myself to remember that fact).

Then I grabbed my I-had-company tray and plunked it onto the island. From the fridge, I snagged my cold cuts that I'd grabbed from the butcher—gourmet salami and black pepper turkey—and cheese I'd picked up from the local dairy—a sharp cheddar, a pepper jack, and a small wheel of yummy brie that was mild and delicious and melted in my mouth. I had to stop myself from eating the entire thing every time I bought it. I grinned, set my cheese knife next to it. Which was why I only bought it for Game Night festivities. Aside from the cheese and meat, I also had some cookies and pastries from the bakery downtown that I'd picked up earlier that morning. I loaded them onto the tray then poked my head back into the fridge and snagged the basket of strawberries Eloise had given me that needed to be eaten soon, otherwise they would go bad. It only took a couple of minutes to wash them and cut off the tops, and then I sliced an apple for good measure.

All to allow myself some time and space to think about how to best handle the woman in the other room.

Genuine or not?

Trying to make a point?

About what, though? That she came in peace? Or that she wanted Joel?

I wasn't sure. Which was why I was spending a few extra moments fanning the apple slices and retrieving a little ramekin for honey, topping it up with a spicy-sweet variety that was beyond addicting.

Then—even though I was no closer to answers—I knew I'd dawdled enough. So, I picked up the tray and carried it, along with a couple of plates, into the family room, placing everything on the table.

"I—" Willow began.

"I just need to grab the wine," I chirped, determined to be mannerly.

"I don't want to be—"

I stopped, glanced back, and held her eyes. "It's no trouble. *You're* not any trouble." Then before I could feel guilty for driving the point I was clinging to home (the one I was desperate to hold on to because if I started to worry about Joel still having feelings about her again, I'd tarnish what we'd shared at the festival), I bustled back into the kitchen. Snagging the glasses, the wine opener, and one of the chilled bottles of white from my favorite Napa Valley winery from the fridge. A breath and I moved back to the family room, perching next to Willow on the couch and pouring us each a glass of wine.

"Now," I said, handing her glass over and picking up one of the tarts I'd set out—this one a lemon custard with a blueberry cheesecake swirl that was to die for.

I took a bite.

Buckled down and channeled my Mayoral Magic.

"You wanted to apologize."

TWELVE

JOEL

"I hope your woman got busy in the kitchen today," Fox said, loping up the stairs in a way that should have been impossible with his big, hulking body.

"She had meetings all afternoon, man," I told him, having done my usual that morning before heading to the rink.

Peeping into her planner.

My woman was busy and worked her ass off and writing in her planner helped her organize her thoughts.

Lucky for me, she didn't give a fuck if I looked at her schedule, as long as I didn't mess up her spread.

Of stickers and color-coded washi tape and writing.

Though, I *could* get away with adding the occasional sticker— so long as it was one of the ones I'd had printed for her.

That morning I hadn't needed to.

She'd already placed us in her evening hours, along with a decorative border of blue that was close to the Rush colors—but not the tape I'd special-ordered for her.

Tape she'd launched over a hillside.

Remind me not to piss off my woman again.

Thankfully, I didn't have any other not-so-ex wives.

Thankfully, the girl who owned the Etsy store knew me by name and had been all too happy to take my money when I'd reached out that morning to order more.

Fox groaned as he reached the stairs, dropping his hands to the small of his back and arching dramatically. "These fucking stairs, man."

"The rebuild on my house is almost done," I reminded him with a roll of my eyes. "Then you'll have a sum total of three stairs to reach my front door."

"Thank fuck for small miracles."

"Weren't you just the one who was going on and on about how you were a prime physical specimen?" I pointed out.

"*On* the ice," Fox grumbled. "With blades strapped to my feet and a minimally friction-filled surface." He stretched again, back popping like bubble wrap. "*Then* I'm a prime physical specimen."

"Of what?"

I whirled to see Dessie bouncing up the stairs, wearing jeans and a Monroe's T-shirt, her long, sleek ponytail swaying behind her, seemingly unbothered by the flight of steps Fox had just been bemoaning.

Fox waggled his brows. "Of man, baby. I'm a prime physical specimen of a *man*. A big, sexy—"

"Oh," she said, her expression way too innocent as she tapped a finger on her bottom lip. "I thought you were going to say you were a prime physical specimen of idiocy."

Fox clamped a hand over his heart. "Jesus, Dessie. Nothing like coming in with the guns hot. Are you *trying* to wound me?"

"Just your ego." A shrug, lips curved into a smirk. "Because if I was really trying to wound you, I'd mention that beard dye you used to cover up all your gray hairs."

He gasped. "How dare you!"

A toss of her long, black ponytail. "Oh, I dare. I *live* to dare, princess."

Fox's eyes narrowed, a flash of something that wasn't his usual joking demeanor darting through his expression as he stepped closer to Dessie. "You—"

I jabbed my key into the lock and opened the door, ordering them to, "Save the shit talk for board games, yeah?"

They were less than a foot apart, eyes locked on each other.

My question had them jumping apart...and my lips twitching, knowing I had some gossip to share with my Rosie girl.

Though she'd probably already clocked the tension.

My woman didn't miss much.

"After you, Des," I began as Fox straightened and walked forward without sparing another gaze at Dessie, moving in through the hall—

Then stopping abruptly.

My hand was flat against the door, holding it open as I watched Dessie come in, but I caught the motion, started to turn back.

And froze.

Because Willow was on my couch again.

Holding a glass of wine. A charcuterie board sat on the table in front of her.

"Um," Fox muttered. "Care to explain the strange woman on your couch?"

"Joel!" Willow hopped to her feet, rounded the coffee table, and hurried up to us.

"Willow," I said, trying to keep my tone even. "How'd you get in?"

"Billie Rose." A glance over her shoulder, toward the kitchen, and I heard the sound of water running. "She's just making me some tea."

A soft hint of orange.

Dessie coming in.

Willow's expression cooled slightly.

"Who's that?" Dessie said, just as frostily, clearly picking up on the odd vibes Willow was putting out.

Narrowed eyes. Willow's face turning ugly. Her chin came up, lips pursed, brows furrowed. "*I'm* Joel's wife." Her chin lifted further. "Who are *you?*"

But Dessie had gone still.

Along with Fox.

And, really, their expressions would have been comical if I wasn't so pissed at Willow. Billie was here. Billie had welcomed her in with wine and food—I wasn't an idiot; I knew what was on the table, knew it showed my Rosie had been being hospitable (and maybe trying to ply her with alcohol to get her to open up).

Well, Willow was open—openly hostile.

She was also full of shit—and was spreading that shit far and wide.

Wife.

That was two fucking times too many for her to pull that fucking card, especially with how it had hurt Billie before.

"Willow is my *ex*-wife," I supplied quickly as Fox spun slowly to face me, his mouth agape. "She made it very clear she wanted to be an ex."

Fox's brows went up.

Dessie choked.

"Five years ago."

The water turned off in the kitchen.

"Apparently, there was an issue with the paperwork making the ex part official," I said, glancing back at Willow and seeing her cheeks flush. *Good,* I thought, fury bubbling in my stomach, already beyond done with this shit. "She's here in River's Bend to fix it."

"She had to come here for that?" Dessie asked.

I flicked my gaze to Dessie's, saw she was already reading the situation correctly.

"Yup," I muttered. "Luckily, she's going to *fix it*"—I glanced back at Willow held her eyes—"so she can move on with her life and Billie and I can move on with ours."

That flush disappeared. In fact, her skin went very, *very* pale.

Good.

Maybe she'd cool it with this shit.

"Huh," Fox said, drawing my focus for a beat. "I thought lawyers dealt with legal problems that needed fixing."

I slanted another glance at Willow. "Me too."

Silence.

Awkward. Tense. Cold.

Then footsteps were coming from the kitchen, and Billie Rose moved into the hallway. I braced, worried about the storm that might be coming my way, expecting hurt and more anger and...for Billie to be looking for another excuse to run.

Instead, she came right up to me, slipping her arms around my waist, rising on tiptoe to brush her mouth over mine. "I thought I heard you," she murmured.

I settled my hand on her jaw, her cheek, tilting her head up. "You good?" I asked, searching her eyes.

Her palm covered my hand. "Fine, honey," she whispered, brushing her mouth over mine.

My fingers flexed when she would have dropped back onto her heels. "You sure, sweetheart?"

"Promise." She spun in the circle of my arms, voice lifting. "I was actually just putting some water on for tea." A flick of her stare up to mine, eyes sparkling. "I invited Willow to stay for board games." A beat. "I figured we needed to show her our special brand of River's Bend hospitality."

Now *I* was certainly the one with the comical expression on my face.

"Umm," Fox muttered, giving me wide eyes.

"Just because Joel and Willow are over doesn't mean that we

can't all be friends." Billie batted her eyes at me. "Isn't that right, honey?"

It was my turn to say, "Umm."

She smiled. "Exactly." A tilt of her head, the kettle beginning to whistle. "There's the hot water. Come in everyone! I've already got food on the table." She spun on her heel, disappeared back into the kitchen, calling "Get eating!" over her shoulder as she went.

Silence. Again.

Still awkward and tense and...well, it wasn't cold any longer, but it sure as shit wasn't comfortable.

Never one to let that faze him, Fox turned to Willow. "So, are we playing Nerts or UNO?"

"I...um..." Willow's stare came to mine, darted away—toward the kitchen, to Fox, to Dessie. Then to the front door.

I felt her prepare to escape before she'd even taken the first step.

And I didn't bother to stop her when she slipped past Fox, past me, past Dessie, and yanked the door open.

"I have to go," she said, as she was halfway over the threshold.

Then the door was swinging shut, closing with a slam.

Dessie looked from the now shut door then back at us, her brows lifted to sky-high proportions.

"I guess that means she's not staying for board games?"

THIRTEEN

BILLIE ROSE

"Sooo," Dessie said after I'd dumped the water out of the kettle—since none of us were going to drink tea when there was wine and beer available.

"So," I repeated, scooping up some brie onto a piece of bread and dousing it in honey.

And avoiding the obvious.

And thinking that I owed both my niece *and* Dessie an apology for being so nosy and involved and meddling in her life.

Being on the other end of that was...

Sigh.

"Sooo," she said again, reaching for a pastry. "Do you care to elaborate on the fact that Joel has a *wife?*"

There was a thread of anger in her voice, something I appreciated as a friend clearly having my back and being upset for me that the man I loved had a freaking *wife*, but...I also heard the hurt.

That I hadn't shared something this big with her.

That I'd kept her out of my life when I'd needed a friend.

And, look, I might have *tried* to do that, to lock it down and pretend. I was damned good at it. Until Joel. The man had torn down my walls and left me vulnerable and open and...trying to be emotionally healthy.

Ugh.

But I also needed her to know that I hadn't wanted to keep this from her—and I know I wouldn't have been able to, anyway, because she would have sniffed it out in a matter of minutes. It was just dumb luck and timing that Joel had gotten to me first, and that I'd been busy with setting up and hadn't gotten a lot of face-to-face time with my friend.

Still, I told her, "We just found out about Willow the night before the Wildflower Festival."

"You waited two whole days to tell me?" she said, but her tone was light.

"Sorry." I squeezed her hand.

"It's good, honey." She squeezed back.

"Sex Hair!" Fox blurted, nearly making me drop my cheese.

I froze then narrowed my eyes at him, tightening my grip so I could keep hold of my brie. "Not cool, man," I muttered.

"It's why she had Just Been Fucked Hair at the festival." Fox lifted a fist, waited for Joel to bump it, and when he didn't, he was nonplussed, just dropped it to his side and kept blabbering. "You really *did* take a page out of the Fox Brown book of conflict resolution."

Joel sighed and glanced at me. "Sorry, Rosie."

I nudged his thigh with mine, pressing close then keeping it there, keeping the contact, keeping close so he knew I wasn't upset. If anything, for whatever reason it was when it came to dealing with one Fox Brown, I was amused.

His book of conflict resolution.

Just Been Fucked Hair.

Lord, the man never stopped talking.

Dessie, though, as was usual when dealing with big, brash Fox, wasn't amused. She rolled her eyes and huffed out a sigh. "Nice," she muttered. "My friend was hurting, and you're talking about orgasming her into submission."

"Is there a *better* way to get over a sore heart?"

"Sore something," Dessie said under her breath.

"Yeah, baby cakes, you'd be sore because I'm so big you'd—"

She snorted, rolled her eyes. "Big." A scoff. "Yeah, *princess*, you've got a big head. The only trouble is that it's the wrong head that's big."

Fox's eyes narrowed. "I'll have you know I'm a prime physical specimen—"

"Of another fuckboy who's too wrapped up in his own dick to understand what a woman actually wants," Dessie snapped.

His chest puffed up. "I know what a woman wants." He leaned in close, so close that I didn't think either of them remembered that Joel or I were there. Not right then. Not with every bit of their focus on each other.

Dessie's chin came up. "Oh, do you?"

His hand dropped onto the table, right between her knees, and swear to God, if he swept that hand across the wooden surface, knocking the dishes and remaining food to the floor, then reached over and lifted Dessie onto the table, climbed on top of her, I wouldn't be surprised.

Or upset.

Mostly because I'd finished off my brie.

But also because this shit—this *chemistry*—was hotter than porn.

I glanced up at Joel, saw he was watching them just as closely.

"What are you so afraid of?" Fox asked and it was a quiet, dangerous question that drew my gaze, my focus.

Because Dessie had come back to River's Bend two years before after having gotten the promotion she'd always dreamed about—lieutenant at a big city fire department. Only she hadn't come back to River's Bend the same starry-eyed girl with a fire lit under her, ready to take on the world.

She'd come back broken.

"Nothing," she whispered. "I'm not afraid of anything."

Fox bent closer, his hand now on the edge of the couch, placed smack dab on the cushion...directly between Dessie's thighs.

I sucked in a breath.

Hot. This was H.O.T.

And also concerning. Yup. I was very concerned and watching my friends so closely because I was very, *very* concerned about their mental well-being.

"Liar," Fox taunted, leaning even closer.

The air grew taut, and neither of them moved.

I pressed my thighs together, leaned back against Joel. "Okay, sweetheart." His voice was silken heat in my ear and so soft I had to strain to hear it. "Time to stop looking at my teammate like he's a Hemsworth."

I looked up at my man, mouthed, "I'm not."

His teeth on my earlobe. "Liar." A taunt and, yup, that soft puff of heat on my ear was hot as hell.

"I'm *not*," I whispered.

"Later," he murmured. "You're going to be in so much trouble *later.*"

I shivered.

Joel felt it, his teeth grazing my skin once more before he straightened.

I couldn't wait for that trouble. He'd take it out on my ass and...I'd enjoy every second of it.

Grinning, I focused back in on the scene in front of me—and my stomach soured when I took in Dessie's expression. The real one that was hidden beneath the bravado and the fire she was tossing at Fox.

There was fear—*real* fear in my friend's eyes.

"Nerts!" I all but shouted, stuffing a cracker in my mouth and talking around it. "I want to play Nerts!"

Fox went so still I wasn't even sure he was breathing.

Then he slowly lifted his hand, and for a second, I thought he was going to plunge it into Dessie's hair, to draw her close, to kiss her—or maybe take his shot at orgasming her away from heartbreak.

But instead, after a long moment, he sat back, his hand going to the arm of the chair he was sitting in, clenching tight, muscles and tendons standing out in sharp relief.

The room was silent.

The tension was still palpable.

Then Dessie pursed her lips and glanced at the clock.

Uh-oh. Escape route activated.

"Actually, I should head back to Monroe's," she said, seeming to deliberately lean in close to Fox and snagging another piece of salami as though to prove to herself—and maybe Fox—that she could be close to him and remain unaffected.

The liar, all the way around.

"We have a delivery coming in the morning." She shoved the salami in her mouth. "I need to get ready for it."

"Liar." Another taunt. One that was a whisper and yet gunshot loud.

Dessie's cheeks went bright pink, but she didn't acknowledge Fox—or his whisper. She just stood and rubbed her hands on her jeans, glancing toward me. "I'll catch you tomorrow?"

My eyes flicked to Fox, who'd tensed, and I could almost see him launching himself out of that chair and pinning Dessie to the floor. *Yum.*

"Trouble," Joel murmured again, fingers grazing my arm.

I pinched his thigh.

"Dessie," I began gently.

My friend backed up a step even as she determinedly kept her gaze directed away from the big, brooding hockey player, something that had Fox's hands clenching so tightly on the chair's arms, I was surprised it didn't call out in protest.

But it wasn't until I saw his legs flex, his body start to rise off the cushion that I enacted evasive maneuvers.

"Willow said she was moving to River's Bend!"

Dessie's eyes went wide, and her gaze ricocheted between me and Joel.

Then she sank back onto the couch.

And Fox's hands relaxed.

Fourteen

God, I loved this woman.

Or maybe I was seriously afraid of her.

Or maybe...it was more the second than the first.

Okay, no. I loved her, and I especially loved how fucking brilliant she was.

Willow stood, arms akimbo, expression befuddled outside the apartment door. "I don't understand," she murmured, brows drawing together as she focused on the keys in her hand and then up at the door. Then at Billie. Then...at me.

I slipped an arm around Billie's shoulders and drew her close. "Rosie mentioned you were moving to town."

"Yes," Billie grinned up at me. "Isn't it great?"

Great *acting*, maybe.

"And the town has a program for temporary accommodations." She plucked the keys out of Willow's hand, used them to unlock the door, and pushed it open.

The apartment was furnished—which didn't surprise me. The fridge was also probably full, if I knew anything about my Rosie.

"This space is yours for the next month," Billie said, sweeping an arm out and leading Willow down the hall. "That will hopefully give you enough time to find a place and work out a move-in date. Don't worry, though," she added chipperly. "If you need some extra time, I know a few people." A wink. "Okay, the kitchen is through here." She walked into the room and tugged open the fridge. "And there's some groceries to get you started..."

Knew it.

"...and the bathroom is just through here."

I watched Willow follow her woodenly down the hall and felt a blip of guilt for her having gotten the full Billie Rose treatment.

Then I thought about the way she'd introduced herself to Dessie as my wife.

And Billie's face on the hillside.

That blip of guilt disappeared so quickly I wasn't even sure it had existed in the first place.

"The utilities are up and running, and don't worry"—she spun and squeezed Willow's arm—"I've got them covered until you're on your feet again."

Willow's mouth opened.

Closed.

And I didn't know what the hell was going on with my ex, but I did know she'd been bested.

Especially when there was a knock at the door just as Willow opened her mouth to reply.

"Oh," Rosie said, her fingers brushing mine as she moved past me to answer it, "that'll be the rest of it."

"What's *the rest of it?*" Willow asked.

I grinned, leaned back against the wall. "No clue."

———

The rest of it had been clothes and linens and a revolving door of River's Bend's best meddlers.

"I don't know whether to swat that lush ass of yours," I said, sweeping my hand down her back, fingertips dancing at the bottom of her spine, "or to pin you against the wall and kiss you senseless."

Her breathing hitched, footsteps faltering as she began heading for my car.

But my Rosie had spine.

She glanced up at me, the barest hint of pink gathering on her cheekbones. "Or, you could do both."

My fingertips danced above that ass I loved. "Yeah?"

She shivered. "Yeah."

I moved, stepping close, arm moving, palm flying through the air—

Smack!

"You didn't!" she gasped.

I sure as fuck did. Just like I grabbed her and pinned her against the side of my car—since there wasn't a wall—the next moment, coaxing her legs around my waist and leaning into her soft body, loving the way her curves melted against me, how her hands came to my chest, not to push me away but to dig her nails in and keep me close.

"I did," I murmured, bending and pressing my lips to her throat. I inhaled, searing that tart and sweet and floral mix that was Billie's own into my senses, then straightened and looked back into her eyes. "You've been busy, Rosie baby."

Her gaze slid to the side then returned to mine. "Yeah."

"Want to clue me in on what else you have in store?"

Teeth pressing into her bottom lip, there and gone in an instant, but still calling to my dick. This was probably a bad idea, holding her like this in a public place where anyone could see us, where Willow could see us, where her parents might drive by, where Fox or the guys might do the same.

Gossip and shit-giving and annoying parents and exes.

All bad.

But I didn't care.

Not with her body pressed to mine, not with her ass in my hands. "*Why* have you been busy, sweetheart?"

An inhalation.

"Tell me, Rosie."

She released her breath. "Like I told you guys last night, she showed up and wanted to apologize, but she was being weirdly possessive for an ex, saying she is going to fix what went down with the divorce, and that was *before* the scene with Dessie in the hallway. She *said* she wanted to apologize." Rosie shrugged. "But anyway it didn't really matter why she was there at our apartment again. I'd already decided at that point."

I smoothed back her curls. "Decided what?"

"To give her some River's Bend hospitality."

My brows dragged together.

Billie's hand lifted, gently smoothing the furrow between them out. "There's something going on with her, and yeah, I don't know her, but I can see at least that much. And you said it yourself, this isn't the Willow *you* knew five years ago."

"No, she's not the woman I knew. Not really."

"So"—she blew out a breath—"like I told you last night, she apologized. Full stop, said she was sorry that she hurt my feelings, and I accepted."

"Sweetheart," I began.

Rosie shook her head. "I mean, what was I going to do? Make things even more awkward and tense by refusing to accept it?" She shrugged again. "No, of course not. It wouldn't help us deal with any of this. So, when she didn't have anywhere to go, I decided on River's Bend hospitality."

I tugged at a curl. "But, Rosie baby, that's a little far, even for you. She's my wife—or says she is"—I really needed to talk to an attorney—"and I'm in a relationship with *you*. She's not your responsibility."

"Look, from what I see, there are three possibilities." Rosie began ticking them off on her fingers. "She really has nowhere to go and needs River's Bend to be her safety zone, she's trying to get you back, or she's in town to mess with your life." Rosie shrugged, curves brushing my body with the movement. "If it's the first, I'll make sure she has a safe spot to land because that's what *I* need to do to be happy in my soul. I help people, even if I don't like them. And if it's the second or third, I'm keeping that bitch close enough so she doesn't get the chance to take her swing at you."

My breath caught, pulse speeding up. "Sweetheart," I began again.

"Hush, now, honey." Her fingers ran through my beard, tips just brushing my skin. "I told you that I'm going to do better, and that means having your back like you've had mine."

Fuck. Now my throat was tight.

Her fingers pressed again, tilting my head down, meshing our gazes. "I'm here. I'm not running." Her palm flattened. "And if that means I have to help someone in need, I'm good with that."

Of course she was.

She was Billie Rose.

"And," she went on, "if that means I'm keeping a would-be enemy closer while the lawyer I put on retainer this morning does her magic, then"—a shrug—"I'm good with that too."

Fuck, I loved this woman.

I leaned in, brushed her nose with mine. "You didn't have to do that."

"I know," she whispered. "But I wanted to."

"Billie Rose magic," I whispered back.

"I've been thinking of it as Mayoral Magic."

My lips curved. Of course she did. And the words just flowed out of me. "You're so fucking beautiful you take my breath away."

She went still, eyes wide, lips parted.

"Here, Rosie baby," I murmured, covering the spot over her heart. "And here." Brushing my knuckles over her temple. "And, of course, *here*." My hand cupping that ass I loved so much. "So beautiful. So smart. So lucky to have you as mine."

Her exhale was shaky. "Joel."

"So lucky to be able to hold and touch and fuck you."

"*Joel*."

"And kiss and talk and breathe the same fucking air as you."

She rested her forehead against mine.

"I'm going to kiss you now," I told her. "Even though Fox will somehow find out about it and give me shit for it in the locker room."

Now her lips tipped up. "Worth it?"

"Definitely."

And then I did kiss her, tasting that mouth and taking my time with it, not caring who was watching or the crap I'd get if someone saw me playing kissy face on the side of the road. It was just me and the woman I loved.

Just me and Rosie together.

Just me and Rosie figuring out our shit.

"Joel?" she asked softly when we broke apart, her blue irises melted icebergs as she stared up at me.

"Yeah?"

Her eyes flicked to the side, and I followed her stare, saw that Willow was standing at the railing of her apartment, watching us.

Fucking weird.

But my Rosie just laughed and smirked up at me.

"I wonder what she'll say about the welcome party."

FIFTEEN

Okay, so a welcome party for Joel's ex-wife was probably a bit much.

But...I'd decided.

Over cheese and wine and insecurities, I'd made a decision. I could keep feeling like shit, could keep feeling unworthy and unsure, could let those emotions eat away at me until I did something stupid again (like run away from a future I wanted), or I could do my level best to support the man I loved...*and* keep an eye on the woman I wasn't sure had his best interests in mind.

So really, there was only *one* choice.

Mayoral Magic.

A Billie Rose special.

Be nosy as fuck and intrusive and...meddle until my heart was content—or safe, anyway.

Willow didn't have anywhere to go? I could fix that.

Willow didn't know anyone in town aside from Joel and now me? I could also fix that.

With a party. With a bunch of people coming to her place, all introducing themselves and forging bonds and saying—

"You're Joel's ex-wife, right?"

Heh.

Because gossip traveled fast.

Was I patient zero of the gossip plague? Maybe.

But it was effective. The question stopped Willow from introducing herself as Joel's wife and I hadn't heard her try to summon up a protest to the title of *ex* for at least—I glanced down at my watch—twenty minutes.

Progress.

An arm wound around my middle, and I glanced up, saw my niece, Bailey looking down at me. "Someone has some explaining to do."

I didn't bother to fight her when she drew me away from the festivities (and away from keeping watch of a certain *willowy* blonde), nor when she drew me out onto the causeway, having paused only to snag two hard seltzers on the way.

She shoved one toward me once we were far enough away from everyone else, then cracked the top of hers. "Tell me everything."

"I—"

"No bullshit, Billie," she said, rightfully cutting me off.

Because it was true. I'd been about to give her a load of bullshit.

"Willow is his ex-wife. Except not."

Bailey's face changed, and she leaned in. "Joel is *married?!*" she hissed.

Unfortunately.

"They filed the paperwork," I said. "He signed and sent it all off, but she told his lawyer that they'd changed their minds." I sighed. "And Joel didn't know. And then he didn't check because... of shit going on with his life, including that she'd hurt him by demanding the divorce in the first place, and he was traded a couple of times. So, in between the moves, he never checked to see if the paperwork came through."

Bailey's expression turned disbelieving. "He never checked on his divorce."

"I know," I said. "Believe me, I *know*. But that happened and now we're here, five years later, and she showed up at the apartment calling herself his wife."

"Oh, honey," Bailey murmured, taking my hand and squeezing it tight.

I squeezed back, forced a smile. "Not my happiest moment, for sure."

"Shit, what a mess."

"Yeah."

A disapproving look. "Also, you've been holding out on me."

"Just to say, Queen of Holding Her Cards Close to Her Chest" —Bailey winced—"this all just happened a couple of days ago."

Bailey exhaled. "And that matters because you would have been open to sharing it all, Miss I Can Handle My Own Shit?"

Now *I* winced. "Okay, so maybe we both come by it naturally."

"Damn right, we do." She tapped her can against mine. "Cheers, baby."

I swatted at her.

She nudged my shoulder, sipped, and asked, "So what are you going to do?"

"About what?" I couldn't resist teasing, wanting to hold on to the lighter mood her cheers had wrought, not wanting to sink back into the hurt and worries.

The look she shot me...

I grinned, sipped from my own can. Then I sighed, gave her that serious anyway. "I mean, keep doing what I'm doing, I guess. Joel's made it clear he's done with her, that he wants to be with me, and...I believe him."

Bailey's face softened. "Good," she whispered.

"So, I'm treating it like I'd treat any problem."

"Billie Rose magic," Bailey said, mouth curving.

My lips twitched. "*Mayoral* Magic."

Laughter, then a nudge of her shoulder. "And also maybe a dash of keeping my enemy close?"

That had my amusement fading and I couldn't deny the sentiment, shrugging and saying, "I mean, you got a look at her. She's beautiful and maybe wants to stay married to the man I love—" I stopped, clenched my teeth together, but the words were out there, were in the air and in not my head and Bailey had heard.

My niece sucked in a breath then exhaled slowly. "You love him."

I seriously considered chugging the seltzer, if only to avoid having this conversation.

"Billie."

The can protested under my hand, a little dent forming in its side.

Bailey bumped my shoulder again. "I'm happy for you," she whispered. "He's a good guy."

He was. The *best* guy.

"But still," she advised, "take your time. Enjoy the ride. Keep your heart open."

I glanced up, admitted, "I almost messed things up when Willow showed up."

"Understandable." She bumped me again. "And look where you are now, honey. You're here and he can't keep his eyes off you" —a tilt of her head and my gaze followed, saw Joel standing and talking to Ryan, but Bailey was right, he *was* watching me—"so I think that says enough about where you guys are going."

I waved, belly warming when he waved back. "Yeah?"

"His love is written in every line of his body."

"I'm scared," I whispered. "I feel so much for him. It's like standing on a cliff and trying to get the nerve to jump into the river below."

"I get that."

I knew she did. Because she'd jumped herself not that long before.

"Yeah." My gaze drifted back to Joel's, held.

"Billie?"

I looked back at my niece. "Yeah?"

"The jumping—when you finally feel ready to do it—is the best part."

My heart skipped a beat and my eyes burned, but I held it together, cupping Bailey's jaw. "I am so fucking proud of you." She'd come so far. Was such an amazing and strong and wonderful person.

Her eyes welled.

My vision went blurry.

Then she blew out a breath, leaned in and quickly kissed my cheek. "No more sappy stuff." Her mouth curved. "Otherwise, we'll have two broody hockey players over here worried about their women crying."

I laughed. "Fair point."

"Damn right, it is." She tapped her can to mine again. "Okay, now spill all the tea. What's this I hear about a petition to change the landscaping at the high school?"

I sighed, happy for my niece—but also happy to let the serious-ness of the moment go—and tipped my head back. "The school district wants to go drought tolerant and native"—something I agreed with, considering that our town had burned down a year ago—"and the parents are concerned that there won't be enough green space for the kids to run around on."

Her brows tipped together. "Have times changed so much that high school kids are running around during the school day?"

I knew what she meant.

Bailey hadn't gone to school in River's Bend—she'd only spent the summers here with her grandparents. But I imagined her high school experience was much like mine. We'd hustled to classes, schlepping backpacks that were way too heavy, and had spent our lunch periods crammed into tables or the couple of benches that were in the shade.

We weren't running across the quad playing tag or having four square tournaments.

I shrugged. "They still have the track and football field," I told her. "And a soccer field. And way more trees and even an outdoor shade structure. It's just that the quad is more outdoor garden than stretch of green sod."

"Which seems reasonable," Bailey said. "Shade. Benches. Plenty of places to sit and giggle with friends or to cuddle up to their respective partners and try to sneak a kiss."

"God," I muttered. "Do me a favor and don't mention that last part to anyone else." I rubbed my forehead. "I'm getting a headache just thinking of the outrage."

"Everyone in town seems a little on edge," she said softly. "The petition and I've heard the school board meetings have been intense. Plus, the Rants and Raves group on social media has been busier than I've ever seen it."

It had been busier than *I'd* seen it too.

People's tempers were short.

Patience was thin.

We were still seeing lots of support, but it was...different.

"Ever since the fire," I murmured, "things have been a little tense. It's like something was broken and even though we're all trying to fix it, it'll never be the same."

Bailey squeezed my hand. "We lost people."

"Yeah," I whispered.

Some had died. Some had moved away and would never be back.

My town had changed, and while I was trying to make sure that any coming out of that were for the better, I had to admit, I wasn't sure I could pull that off.

Wasn't sure it *would* be better.

"You'll fix it," Bailey said, coming close and resting her head on my shoulder. "You'll fix it, and you'll make River's Bend better than ever. I know you will."

That was just the thing.

I wasn't sure I would.

Sixteen

Joel

"Um," Billie murmured a couple of days later. "This isn't the way to our apartment."

It wasn't.

And, frankly, I was surprised that it had taken this long for her to notice. Though, I chalked it up to the school district meeting that had run long.

Progress was happening between the parents and the high school's landscape plan.

But my Rosie had needed to wade in.

Something I didn't like. But my Rosie was my Rosie and people looked to her for solutions, for support, to get things done, and as long as she liked it, I wasn't going to intervene. I *was*, however, going to redirect and make sure she got enough sleep and mental rest and—

Hell, I was going to fuck her senseless, pin her to the bed, and make sure she passed out for at least eight hours.

Then I'd fuck her again, let her take a shower, feed her, and *maybe* let her out of my sight.

Because I'd played tonight and I'd done my post-game and I'd cooled down and showered, changed, and driven to the apartment.

And she'd still been at work.

So, I'd turned around, gone to City Hall, and spotted her car in the lot.

The meeting had finished, but she was speaking to a few concerned parents outside the council room as I walked up to her.

A conversation she didn't finish as I hooked an arm around her middle and hauled her away.

Thankfully, I knew the people she'd been speaking to, so they hadn't been upset that I'd interrupted their conversation. They'd just waved as I herded her to my car.

Hers was still at City Hall.

Another portion of my evil plan, muahaha!

Because, as she'd just realized, we weren't going to the apartment.

"Joel?"

I signaled and turned right down the slightly curving road, the streetlights few and far between out on this side of town.

Because most of the houses were still being rebuilt.

But not mine.

Mine was done. And Rosie's. Because it had become as much hers as it had mine during the rebuild.

"No, Rosie baby," I told her, eyes on the road, practically feeling her vibrate with impatience as she waited for me to answer. "We're not heading to the apartment."

More vibrating.

Mostly because that answer hadn't been satisfactory.

But I didn't expand on it, just glanced over at her, grinned, and returned my focus to the road.

"Okay," she grumbled. "Well, if we're not going to the apartment, where are we—"

She inhaled sharply.

Because I was turning into our driveway.

"Honey," she whispered. "Are you fucking kidding me?"

I hit the clicker, grinned at her again, then pulled forward into the now-open garage. "No, Rosie baby," I said, turning off my car and popping the door. I hopped out, rounded the hood, and got to hers just as she was stepping out.

"You didn't tell me," she whispered.

"I wanted it to be a surprise."

Her hand came to my cheek, pressed lightly into my skin. "Your house."

I covered her hand with my own. "*Our* house. And I know." Then I bent, scooped her up, and started for the door leading inside, ignoring her little squeak of protest as I kicked her door closed.

"What—?"

"Threshold time, sweetheart," I told her, nodding at her to hit the button to close the garage door.

She pressed the button then reached for the knob. "Aren't thresholds supposed to be for the wedding night?"

My heart skipped a beat.

They were.

But I also wanted a million thresholds with this woman, a million nights, a million moments where I could hold her close and she would be mine.

She tugged the door open.

"Don't you think that's where this is leading, Rosie baby?"

The knob slipped from her fingers, slammed shut. "What?" she asked.

I smiled, reached past her, and opened the door, nudging it back with my hip as I carried her inside. "Don't you think that what we have together is leading to that point? That I want to spend the rest of my life with you?"

"I—" She broke off, pressing her lips together, eyes going wide.

"I love you, Rosie baby."

Her nails tightened. "What?"

"I love you."

"What?"

I grinned, carefully extracting those nails from my skin, and continuing to walk into the house. Through the kitchen. Into the hall.

Where my connections—aka Dessie and Bailey had pulled off my request in a way that defied expectations. Battery-operated candles lined the hall, giving the space a soft glow. Flower petals were sprinkled on the floor, a cascade of color leading down the hall.

"Are those candles?" She craned her neck, head swiveling. "Wait. Joel. Are those candles?"

"They're battery-operated," I told her, in case she was worried about the fire risk (a legitimate concern considering everything that had happened last year).

"But—" She shifted in my arms so rapidly I nearly dropped her as I continued walking. "Wait. And flower petals?" I held her tighter when she shifted again, this time to glance back at me. "When did you have time to do this?"

"I reveal no secrets."

"Bailey and Dessie," she guessed—correctly, though I wasn't going to tell her that. "They weren't at the meeting."

They weren't at the Rush game either.

Because they'd been here.

Sprinkling flower petals and turning on candles and—

"Oh my God! Wait, Joel! Stop walking!" She squirmed in my hold. "Are those stickers?"

They sure were.

Because Bailey and Dessie hadn't just been on flower petal and candle duty. I'd also charged them with scattering the stickers I'd ordered.

But I didn't stop to let Rosie see them.

There would be time for her to look at the plethora of stickers

I'd ordered later, to sort and organize and place them in her planner as she saw fit. *Later.*

Because there was something more important for her to look at *now.*

I stopped at a closed door, the one the candles had been placed in a path directing us toward, turned the handle, and pushed it open.

Her "*Joel!*" was quieter this time, a soft gasp that settled over my skin like the sun on an early spring day.

The candles were here too. On every flat surface and carefully crafted, intricately painted shelf. On the desk that was shaped like an L and built into the space. On the little table I'd picked up from downtown that she'd mentioned liking (but hadn't bought because it was "too expensive"). On the plush rug I'd picked out, knowing she'd love it because it was beyond soft and a mix of her favorite colors. The petals and stickers had been scattered around, dotting the floor, the surface of that desk, the rug, the pair of chairs I'd had the designer buy because I knew that my Rosie would love curling up in them and watching TV or reading or doing her planning.

I set her down gently, waiting until she was steady to release her, hanging back as she walked forward.

Fingertips brushing over the back of those velvet armchairs, along one of the shelves, this one empty, waiting for her to fill it with her planning stuff, her stickers and notebooks and washi tape. Along another that the designer had bought baskets for.

Stopping at the desk.

Where I'd placed a frame that afternoon before I'd gone to the rink.

She spun to face me, and her expression killed me. In the best possible way. Because it wasn't closed down, it wasn't running, there weren't walls and barriers and barbed wire being erected right in front of my eyes.

She was open.

She was mine.

Then she was flying across the office I'd made for her, across the rug and the specialty scrapped hardwood, and leaping into my arms.

Hers went around my shoulders and her mouth came down to mine.

But not before her fingers threaded through my beard and she whispered...

"I love you too."

SEVENTEEN

BILLIE ROSE

I loved the space that he created for me at the apartment.

The piece of home he'd made for me.

This...

This was next level.

This was as though he'd picked and crafted and thought about every detail and then had done his absolute best to make sure it was perfect for me.

Hell, who was I kidding?

There was no doubt he'd done *exactly* that. From the stickers to the flower petals being from pale pink roses (my favorite), to the lilac cabinets and big desk and cozy chairs. The gas fireplace and huge rug and the little round gold table that I hadn't bought from Holly's downtown because I couldn't justify two hundred dollars for a table that was the size of a dinner plate. The baskets on the shelves and the clear acrylic organizers and the bookends and the tiny wooden carving of an oak tree.

And then there was the frame.

Gold and sparkly, and...it took my breath away. Because inside it...were the stickers I'd crumpled and nearly thrown off the hill.

He'd smoothed them out, had framed them, had kept them safe and returned them and—

I spun and ran back to him, any worry and fear at giving this man the last pieces of me disappearing. He already saw everything, already owned every part of me.

Then I was in his arms and the worry was flowing out of me.

"I love you too."

I should have told him the moment I realized where he'd taken me, or when he'd carried me in through the garage, or when he'd all but told me he was going to marry me. I definitely should have told him when he'd said it first, should have ignored the distracting beauty of the candles and petals and stickers and just held him like I was doing now, keeping our gazes locked, our breaths mingling, our bodies meshed together.

I hadn't.

So, I made up for lost time.

"I love you, Joel Marshall. More than my next breath, my next roll of washi, my next—"

His lips hit mine, which was good, because I'd been about to declare that I loved him more than my next...*something*, because the feelings inside me, filling my heart and blood with helium, were so big they were almost indescribable.

His groan rumbled up and his hand was diving into my hair, his big body moving as he brought us to the rug that was as soft beneath my back as it was below my feet. And still he kissed me, still he held me, hand in my hair, the other trailing along my body. His tongue parted my lips, slid inside my mouth, tangled with mine, a hot, sleek dart that teased and whipped my need for him into a frenzy.

I bucked and shoved at his chest, rolling him so I was on top.

He grinned when I sat up, straddling his hips and the hard length of his cock, my hands resting on his pecs. His hot, broad palms settled on my waist, drawing me more tightly against his erection, grinding up against me. "Whatcha doing up there, sweetheart?"

My lips curved. "Just enjoying the sights."

"I'll have you know, my plans for this evening included more fucking and less enjoying of the sights."

"Mmm." I bent, buried my face in his throat, teeth lightly gripping one of the tendons standing out in sharp relief. "Is there even furniture to be doing this fucking thing on?"

His hand tightened in my hair, dragging my teeth from his skin, locking those deep green eyes onto mine. "Did you miss the desk?"

I shook my head.

"Or the chairs?"

"No, honey," I breathed, mind reeling with the images of him bending me over that desk, of him fucking me from behind. It would be good—I knew that, had experienced it firsthand. But the chairs, the soft velvet caressing my skin as he stroked into me...that image threatened to turn me to ash.

"Or the rug?"

I suddenly found myself flat on it again, only this time his hands were busy, trailing down my torso, my legs, removing my shoes. I heard them hit—*thunk, thunk*—somewhere behind him but was too distracted to care.

Because his hands were still busy.

Tugging at my clothes.

"I didn't miss the rug, honey," I murmured as those skillful hands had me naked in no time flat then began working on himself, revealing his body in small, delicious increments.

"Good," he murmured. "Because there's another one in the master bedroom."

I shivered. "More of your plans?"

A nip to my lips, my collarbone, his words a hot glaze on my skin. "What do you think?"

"*I* think you need to show me these plans."

"Mmm." His tongue dragging down, lips and mouth circling my nipples, sucking them and nibbling at them and—

"Oh!" I gasped as he bracketed my hands in one of his and brought them over my head, holding me captive as his body—naked and hot and *hard*—came down on top of mine.

"Rosie baby."

My gaze had been drawn down...to the way his hips spread my thighs, to the hard head of his cock brushing my wet pussy.

One arch of my hips and he would be inside.

A rough chuckle and then I was on my belly, pressed into the rug.

Smack!

I jumped, the sting of his palm spreading out like liquid heat.

"This ass," he growled, shifting down and his teeth sinking into his flesh.

I pulled my knees under me.

Another growl.

Glancing over my shoulder, I met his eyes. "Inside me, honey."

He didn't hesitate, just moved close, notched his cock at my entrance and thrust deep.

"*Fuck*," I groaned, my head falling back, hair teasing my shoulders, that stretch, the twinge of discomfort, the mix of pleasure and pain.

Teeth on my shoulder, his big body wrapped around mine.

Fingers stroking my clit, his hot words in my ear.

"I love this wet cunt, love how tight it wraps around my dick, love how it holds me just as tight when I stroke out"—he shifted, sliding almost all the way out of me, the blunt head of his cock stretching my entrance—"and when I push back inside you." He thrust, bottoming out, making my head drop forward, my moans tumbling from my lips. "Hot. Wet." A nip to my earlobe. "*Mine.*"

Already, I was close.

Already, I was ready to stop thinking, to let go, to allow this man to use and abuse and *fuck* my body into oblivion.

"Joel," I whispered, every bit of need in my voice.

"Fuck," he hissed, moving faster, bringing my orgasm closer. "I love it when you say my name like that."

"*Joel*," I groaned as he hit a spot that had stars flashing behind my eyes.

"I love *that*." Faster. Hard. "I love you so fucking much."

"God," I whispered. "Just like that, honey. Fuck me just like —*Oh*," I groaned. "Just like *that*." He was thick and hard, growing harder by the second, pace not faltering, pleasure spiraling. Those stars in my vision were coalescing, spreading out, blinding me. I could see nothing but the pale purple of the rug and those sparks. Could feel nothing but Joel and his heat, his hard cock, his body.

The pleasure he was building in me.

Burning through me.

Exploding.

I screamed, bucking against him, grinding down, that bliss expanding and taking over every inch of my body, filling me with pleasure, locking my muscles as it rolled through me, as it consumed me, as every inch of me went limp.

He was still thrusting, arm around my middle, holding me up as he pounded into me once, twice more.

As his groan echoed in my ears.

As his cock twitched and he came inside me.

We collapsed to the rug, his heat still surrounding me, his body cushioning mine as my eyes slid closed and I just lay there, completely demolished by this man, by his love, by the pleasure he continued to give me day after day after *day*.

A hand down my spine.

Soft, wicked words in my ear.

"How do you like the rug, Rosie baby?"

EIGHTEEN

JOEL

Strictly speaking, sex as a pregame ritual was not advised.

Especially with a doubleheader.

But I'd had three doubleheaders in two days and only one of those was on the ice. My legs should be shot, my body not ready to kick ass at playing hockey. Instead, I was on fucking *fire*.

My legs felt like I could play six games without a break.

My lungs barely felt the dent of my shifts, even if they ran a few seconds longer than they were supposed to.

I was flying—and it was because of the woman who was sitting in the stands, watching me.

My Rosie.

My woman.

My love.

I'd managed to keep her at the house all morning—partly because of those two doubleheaders we'd had in her office and in the kitchen and our bedroom and the shower (our new house was fucking *great*, even if the only rooms with furniture were her office and the master). But I'd also managed to keep her in bed because she was tired and limp with orgasms *and* she'd taken a three-hour nap with me before her cell phone had rung.

I attributed that to Dessie and Bailey working their magic.

I'd dropped my Rosie off at City Hall and she'd done her mayor stuff while I'd gotten ready for the game.

Orgasms. Nap. Woman.

Apparently, *that* was my perfect pregame.

"Nice shift, Joel," Timmy—one of our assistant coaches—said, patting me on the shoulder.

I nodded, focused on the game in front of me. This was some quality hockey tonight, our team having gelled, the playoffs and the hunt for the Calder Cup—the AHL's equivalent for the Stanley Cup—would be beginning soon.

We'd lose some guys to the Gold at some point, as our NHL affiliate began their hunt for the ultimate prize, but for now, we were primed for the remainder of our games, had a full, healthy roster that was working together in a way that we never could have dreamed about at in the beginning of the season, and we were jonesing for some playoff hockey.

This was our time.

I felt that in my bones.

Felt it as much as I sensed something big was coming for me— marriage, babies, a life that wasn't spent out of town half the year and bleeding on the ice.

I loved hockey.

Fucking *loved* it.

But...I was ready to move on.

My eyes slid across the rink, locking onto the shock of blond curls, Bailey and Alex on one side of her, Dessie and Veronica on the other—

No. Dessie and Veronica weren't right next to her.

Not any longer, anyway.

They'd been shifted down one position.

Because there was another blond, her hair straight and sleek under the bright arena lights, sitting next to Billie Rose.

Willow.

My ex—or soon-to-be, I hoped—wife was sitting next to my woman.

Watching me play hockey.

"What the fuck?" Ryan muttered, and seriously, *same*, man. What the fuck was going on in the stands?

Only, it took me a second to process that he wasn't studying the blondes, looking for any sign of strife (or really, any sign that Rosie was upset), but instead, Ryan's focus was on Veronica.

"She and Alex are staying with Bailey at the ranch for the weekend," I said, having become privy to this information when I'd recruited Billie's niece to help me with my plans. "Axel is traveling, and the herd"—literally Bailey's herd of cattle—"needed their vaccinations."

Strictly speaking, Bailey had ranch hands to do that now.

But it wasn't in her nature to sit back and watch someone else work. Plus, Alex was horse crazy, and I figured she found it was an easy way to bond with her stepson.

"Did Veronica's doctor okay that?"

That was information I *wasn't* privy to.

I knew that V had stayed at the ranch while Dessie and Bailey worked sticker and flower petal and candle magic, but I figured it was because she'd needed to watch Alex. He was a good kid—but five going on six—and I suspected the stickers wouldn't have ended up as I'd planned for them if he'd helped with the proceedings.

Stuck on my walls. The mirrors. The trim and doors. Maybe even that expensive rug and table.

Maybe.

Probably.

I glanced back to where he was sitting next to Bailey, his head on her shoulder.

Maybe not.

Regardless, I didn't have an answer to Ryan's question other than, "I think she's allowed to do what she wants, bud."

Ry shot me a glare that should have eviscerated me, but we didn't have a chance to get further into it because the play was shifting, the guys were moving, and then we had to haul our asses over the boards and onto the ice and do that thing called hockey.

Only just as we corralled the puck and started moving into the opposing zone, Ryan peeled off.

Not for an outlet pass.

Not to support the play.

But was skating straight to the glass and pounding on it.

"What the—"

The other team froze for a second and so did I, but this was professional hockey and the whistle hadn't blown...so we continued on, our guys moving the puck to the net and shooting then digging at it for a few seconds until the other team's goalie managed to cover the puck and get a whistle to stop the play.

Bang.

Maybe five seconds had passed.

Bang. Bang. Bang.

But Ryan hadn't stopped banging.

I hauled ass to the boards, to the glass, stomach sinking, getting there just in time to see Ryan grab a linesman's stripes and scream, "Get her some fucking help, yeah?"

Which was when I looked beyond Ry, beyond the players starting to gather at the glass and saw a form crumple...

Dessie tried to grab her, but my Rosie was the one who moved first—of course she did—diving forward, trying to catch Veronica, skin glassy, eyes rolling, lids sliding closed as she slumped forward.

The crowd gasped.

Billie ended up sprawled over Willow and Dessie's legs, arms extended, but—our eyes connected for a second, and I released a relieved breath—her hands were beneath Veronica's head, stopping the other woman's skull from connecting with the concrete floor.

She turned away, barked out an order I couldn't hear over the crowd, whose worried titters were now filling the air, but I saw Dessie nod, extract herself, and then take off. I turned, watching Dessie move, confused when she headed for the door to the rink, yanking at the heavy handle, wondering what in the fuck all she was doing.

Then I realized our trainer, John, one of the team's fully trained medical staff, was making his way across the ice, Fox guiding him with a hand on his arm, steadying him as they reached the boards just as Dessie got them open.

"Joel!"

I jerked back, focused on Billie.

She tilted her head...toward Ryan.

Shit.

"Come on, man," I muttered, snagging his arm, wanting to get him away from the scene, get him back to the bench so he could breathe and refocus and—

Ry shook me off. "Not a fucking chance, Joel," he said, calm and yet icy cold, "and if you fucking try it again, I will drop you to this ice."

Ryan was steady. Even.

A good guy.

But push him far enough, push him on *this*, and I knew he'd do it—and get the drop on me, even with the warning he'd given.

So, I just stood close, shoulder pressed to his, and shut my mouth.

And watched with him.

Watching Bailey hugging Alex and Willow being shoved out of the way to give John some space to work. Watching Billie shifting around, talking to John. Watching their lips move as they exchanged information, even though I couldn't hear a damned thing, couldn't *do* a damned thing.

Except stand there and wait.

For Veronica to open her eyes.

NINETEEN

BILLIE ROSE

"I'm fine," V said, shoving my hand away, pushing away the help.

"Just go slow," I started to advise, but she was already tucking her elbows beneath herself, pressing up to sitting.

"Whoa there," the trainer from the Rush—John—said, grabbing at her shoulder, steadying her.

"I'm fine," Veronica whispered, gaze sliding past us, searching.

"He's with Bailey," I murmured, leaning close and pointing to a spot a few feet away. Maybe I would have taken Alex out of the arena, if I hadn't been catching Veronica, stopping her before she could crack her head against the concrete floor, but I realized after seeing Alex's worried expression that my niece had made the right call.

Let him see his mom was okay.

"Can you help me stand up?"

"Are you sure that's a good idea?" I asked softly. "Just take a minute and make sure you're steady."

Veronica's cheeks were bright pink, her words sharp, but I

knew her annoyance wasn't entirely directed at me when she said, "I have cancer, but I'm not a total invalid."

"You're right, V," I said. "You're not. Still, let's take it slow as we get up, yeah?" Her eyes narrowed, so I pulled out the trump card. "You don't want to scare Alex, right?"

Veronica nodded, cheeks positively blazing. "Right," she whispered.

"Okay, ready? One, two—"

John started to protest, but I glanced down at him, shook my head, and luckily, he got with the program, grabbing her other arm, helping her up to her feet, holding her steady for a moment as she found her balance.

"I'm on a new medication, that's all," she said.

"That's okay," I told her as we shuffled down the aisle sideways, moving between the seats as a trio.

"It makes me dizzy."

"I get that. It takes time for everything to be balanced out." I lightly squeezed her hand as we reached the end of the aisle, nodding at Bailey to lead the way out.

She bit her bottom lip. "Everyone's watching."

They were.

There wasn't any way I could sugarcoat that. Three thousand plus people were watching us, including several dozen who were on the ice and players' benches.

"I know a private place," I said instead. "We'll get you somewhere quiet and sort everything out, okay?"

Her eyes welled. "Not really sure this is something you can sort out, Billie."

"You don't trust in my Mayoral Magic?" I asked lightly, thankful when she laughed, even though it wasn't her normal one. Even though it was more than a little broken and embarrassed and like Veronica had died a little bit inside when she'd fainted in the arena.

I got that.

I'd probably feel the same.

But I was going to do my best to erase that, my best to stop it from happening again—the passing out and the feeling like shit and the embarrassment.

She was a fucking *warrior*, and she was nice and a good mom and it hadn't made for the smoothest of sailing between Bailey and Axel, what with her showing up out of the blue with a five-year-old. But life wasn't smooth, and the circumstances had been complicated and...they were making their own family unit that worked for them.

So, I was on their side.

And it wasn't just because Bailey was my niece and friend.

It was Veronica too. She'd become part of my family too.

"Let's get that privacy," I murmured.

A sigh, but she was nodding, and I knew she felt a little better when she didn't lean on me quite so heavily.

Tap. Tap. Tap.

Our gazes jerked to the ice, to the players who were tapping their sticks on it, who were watching us as we made our way to the exit.

Though, only one was watching in that intensely quiet way of his.

The focus that could come across as both terrifying and... comforting, like the strongest pair of arms pulling a woman close, holding her tight, giving the best hugs ever.

Ryan watched us all the way to the exit, and he continued to watch us through the windows—I knew because I looked as we crossed behind the glass, saw that his teammates had skated away, but that Ry was still watching, Joel by his side.

All the way until we disappeared.

Maybe *after* too. Maybe until the shrill blast of the whistle came, echoing through the rink, faintly reaching my ears.

"Mom!"

I couldn't focus on that, on Ryan and Joel and their worry or the game.

I needed to look after one of my own.

———

The next morning, before the Rush got on a bus and headed off for their next series of games, long after Bailey had bundled Alex and Veronica back to the ranch (and then a few hours after sunup back to San Francisco, despite Veronica's protests), I was walking into a lawyer's office.

With Joel at my side.

Amy Saam came highly recommended, and better yet, she had recently set up her practice in River's Bend.

"What's this I hear about a petition?" Joel asked, as he held the door for me.

I waved a hand. "We got the high schoolers and their parents sorted. A revised landscaping plan is already on the way."

Joel's brows were furrowed. "I thought it was about the green-scape initiative?"

"No," I told him as we moved toward the reception desk, "it's the high school quad and field refurbishment, but that's sorted now."

"Right, but I heard—"

"Can I help you?"

Joel's hand rested on the small of my back, and he glanced up at the woman smiling at us from behind the desk. "We're here to see Amy?"

"Oh!" A glance down at her computer screen. "Joel, right?"

"Yup."

"Great." She stood and moved around the desk, leading us to a conference room down the hall and offering us water or coffee.

Both of us took a coffee—and I knew Joel felt the same as me, that the coffee was a necessary fortification for the conversation ahead, but we'd barely taken a sip before Amy was bustling into the room, a legal pad under one arm, a laptop under the other, a pen tucked into her high brown ponytail. "I'm sorry to keep you waiting," she said, tugging a chair out with her foot and plunking into it. Her stuff hit the surface, she extended a hand, and they exchanged nice-to-meet-yous. Then she got right down to business, recapping what I'd told her on the phone.

"Do I have it all right?" she asked when she'd finished with the divorce timeline and Willow's reappearance, the quick marriage for visa purposes.

I glanced at Joel.

He nodded. "What I don't understand is why she'd come back now."

"Oh," Amy said, flipping a page on the pad. "It's because it's been five years." She kept flipping. "The petition *was* filed."

Joel went still beside me. "Um, what?"

"Yup." Amy opened the laptop, tapped a few keys, and turned the screen to show us the contents. "See? Almost exactly five years ago." A beat. "Well, five years and one month."

"I—" A shake of his head. "But she told me she'd contacted my attorney and canceled it."

Amy chuckled. "You can't really cancel things like this, and my guess is that regardless of what she told you about *changing her mind*, your attorney didn't actually listen to her. The petition was filed, but because she never signed, it's been languishing in the system."

"For five years?" I asked.

Amy nodded. "And after five years, the petition expires."

"Oh shit," I whispered.

"So, I'm still married?" Joel asked.

Another nod. "Now, because this is a unique case, I think we can work it so that the date of separation is five years ago, and she won't have access to your current earnings and property when we refile, but unless you can find a way to get her to sign this time, I would recommend filing for a contested divorce and..."

She kept talking, but my head was spinning.

And so was Joel's, I imagined, as I tried to take in what Amy was saying, and her plan, and the paperwork she would need—

"But"—Joel's hands were clenching the armrests of the chair —"I'm still fucking married."

Amy stopped, and her demeanor softened. "I'm afraid so, Joel, but I can promise that I will get you out of this as quickly as possible, and I will keep digging to find any avenue that will bring this to the conclusion you want as soon as is feasible."

He rubbed his forehead.

"I know this isn't the news you wanted."

Yeah, no shit.

But neither of us said that. Hell, neither of us said much more as she spoke.

Nor when we walked out of the office.

He caught my hand when we'd reached my car, drawing me close, wrapping his arms around my middle. "Fuck, Rosie baby. I'm so sorry about this."

I pulled back, cupped his jaw, his beard tickling my palm. "You have nothing to be sorry for."

He started to protest.

"We will figure this out," I vowed. "Together, yeah?"

His shoulders were stiff, eyes filled with regret and hurt. "I'm —" I kissed him, long enough that he forgot about apologizing, long enough that he pulled me closer.

"Together," I told him when we pulled apart.

His eyes closed, and he brushed his lips over my forehead. "Together," he repeated.

Then I drove him to the rink and kissed him again for good measure, both to distract him from Amy's news and so he wouldn't forget me while he was gone—and also maybe because I liked the way he growled in my ear that I was going to pay for that when he got back. Grinning, I released him and watched him climb onto the bus, waving goodbye as it drove off before heading to the Civic Center for mayor time. I parked behind City Hall, as usual, and then, because Joel's question about the petition hadn't left my mind, even with all that Amy had told us, I popped a head into the superintendent's office to make sure we were on track with the high school's landscape design, and nothing had blown up in the two days since the planning meeting.

Thankfully, everything was proceeding as intended.

But when I got into my office, sat at my desk, and opened my emails...

I saw a message about a petition protesting the greenscape initiative.

Joel was right.

There *was* a growing discontent with the greenscape initiative.

"Christ," I muttered, scrolling the pages.

The fire. Willow. Petitions.

What the fuck was happening to my town?

Twenty

JOEL

God, I hated traveling on the bus.

I was too old to be living out of a backpack, a suitcase, legs crammed into tight seats.

And *this* bus was better than the old ones.

But even with more legroom and not having to share a pair of seats, it still sucked. Trapped for hours, the swaying motion making me slightly queasy and if I took something for the nausea, then my head was fuzzy, like cotton balls had been shoved in my ears.

Look at me go.

Next up, I just needed to mail off my invitations for my pity party for one.

Logically, I knew that a lot of the turmoil in my stomach, my mind, my heart was because of Willow and her deception and the fact that it would take months—at a minimum—to years—if Willow contested—to start my life with Billie.

Finally, I had a future.

And my past was fucking things up.

I sighed, glared out the window, trying to compartmentalize it away, knowing I didn't have control over this situation, knowing that I couldn't even do so much as talk to Willow, to confront her and try to move this shit forward—not with her in River's Bend and me in Nowhere, California, not even able to stare out the window and watch the highway pass by because it was dark and the fog had descended and—

"That's a lot of sighing, man."

I looked over at Fox, lifted my brows in silent question, not wanting to engage.

Not with my current headspace.

"That's all you got?" he asked. "Fuck, Joey boy, you must really be screwed. Did my Billie finally get her head out of her ass and dump you?"

"I guess that means you missed the kiss she laid on him outside the bus," Ryan said.

I shoved a hand through my hair. "She'd be right to break up with me."

Fox and Ryan went still.

Which was the moment I realized I'd been so in my head that I actually said the shit in my mind out loud.

"What the fuck, man?" Fox snapped.

I yanked up my hood, started to turn away, but Fox yanked it back down and grabbed my arm, stopping me.

"*Don't.*"

"Tough shit, Joel. Talk to me."

I huffed out a breath. "And tell you what? That I'm supposed to be divorced, but somehow, I'm not because I didn't follow up on some fucking paperwork?" I laughed but it wasn't amused. "Or maybe I should tell you that the attorney is going to do her best to protect my house so that Willow won't get any of it? Oh, and that the woman I want to marry will have to wait because my ex isn't my fucking *ex?*"

Fox rocked back in his seat, eyes wide.

And congratulations were in order for me, apparently. I'd finally managed to have Fox Brown at a loss for words.

Cue party streamers and confetti and flashing lights.

"Okay," Ryan said, the voice of reason when it was anyone who wasn't Veronica. "Start at the beginning and tell us what the fuck is going on."

I glanced at the fog-shrouded window, so not wanting to have this conversation.

Then back at my friends, as annoying as they were.

And I knew I needed to have it, anyway.

So, I opened my mouth, shoved away the urge to close down, and I told them everything.

The puck flowed from my stick over to Ryan's, landing with a *crack* that echoed across the ice.

Morning skate.

Shaking off the cobwebs and out the sore legs from the bus trip.

We'd practice, eat, nap.

Then get back onto the ice again.

Gear off. Cool down. Shower. Bus. Hotel.

Rinse, repeat for the next three cities.

Then back to River's Bend.

The puck flew back, and I reacted almost without thinking, catching it in the air, tipping it down in the net.

Then turning to snag it from the net, shifting over to a new spot, and passing it back to Ryan, who shot it on the one-time, sending it toward me.

I tipped it again.

Not thinking. Just doing. Over and over again. Switching positions. Shooting and tipping and passing.

Until Ryan called it and skated to the bench, scooping up a water bottle and drinking deeply.

Since I no longer had anyone to pass with—the ice had cleared of our teammates a long time ago—I followed him, taking the bottle from him when he extended it.

"How's the head?" he asked.

I just squirted water in my mouth then dropped the bottle back into the holder. "I'm fine," I muttered once I'd turned away from him, from my teammate who knew that was a lie.

Ry sighed, but didn't comment further, just picked up his stick and asked, "Want to go again?"

I needed to do something that wasn't lying in my hotel room, staring at the ceiling and trying to nap. I needed to punch or check or whale on the fucking puck. "Yeah," I muttered, pushing away from the boards.

I took up position.

Ry snagged some pucks.

We passed and shot until my heart was pounding and my lungs burned and my arms felt heavy enough that lifting my stick was a struggle.

"What you said on the bus was bullshit, you know," he said as we packed it in.

I skated my sorry ass back to the bench. "I know. I can't believe that Willow pulled this shit and—"

A thwack of his stick against my shin guards. "*No*, Joel," Ryan said, "the shit you said about Billie being right to break up with you."

That—

Fuck.

That took me by surprise and my eyes shot to his.

"I don't know what the fuck is going on in your head, and I like Billie, but I know that she couldn't do better than you, man."

I exhaled.

"You're a good person. And a good partner and a good friend and Billie is awesome, but she's also lucky to have you—"

My fingers tightened on my stick. "I was a dick to her when we first met."

"You two were oil and water and she dished it out too. But the more important thing is that you guys sorted your shit, moved past it. So"—another thwack—"nice try, asshole. Give me the next excuse."

I snatched the water bottle, squirted the mix of half Gatorade, half water into my mouth. "That's not a big enough one?"

Joel dropped his chin and looked at me, brows lifted, his not buying my bullshit written itself into his face. "Nope. Sure isn't."

"Then what about the fact that I'm *married?*"

He shook his head, snagged the bottle from me and took a sip.

"Ry—"

"No, man, your time for feeling sorry for yourself is over. Willow is...I don't fucking know—crazy, has ulterior motives, or maybe just realized she seriously fucked up in letting you go and is back to try to fix things now. But she isn't Billie and you're going to sort your shit and you're going to do it because you're a good man and you have a good woman by your side."

My throat went tight. "She left me, Ry."

He stilled. "Billie?"

"No. Willow. And Tammy." I shook my head. "And Jess and Laura. Hell, I even wanted more with Sarah but she told me things weren't going to work out."

Every woman I'd ever been monogamous with.

Every woman I'd loved.

And they'd all left.

Every single one of them.

Ry was quiet for long enough that I was desperate for the superpower to be able to go back in time and pretend I'd never actually said that aloud.

"It doesn't work out until it's the right one."

I gripped my stick tight enough that the composite fibers creaked in protest. "So says the man who was dumped with a ring in his pocket."

Ry went still...and I was a fucking asshole.

"Shit, I didn't mean that. I'm—"

"It's the truth." He shrugged and shook his head. "I thought I'd found forever. I hadn't. But I know I'm worth enough to get that. So, even though things might not have worked out, I know I still deserve happiness." He dropped the water bottle back into the holder, looked up at me with eyes that pierced right the fuck through my soul.

"Have you?"

TWENTY-ONE

BILLIE ROSE

The high school's quad redo.

The greenscape plan.

The water conservation measures.

Kid's soccer.

Books in the local library.

I stared at the stack of petitions sitting on my desk and wondered what the fuck was going on, barely hearing the Rush game playing on my computer, the radio announcer talking quickly as he described each play my guys were completing.

But I wasn't really processing the game.

Not when it was late, and another email had hit my inbox.

A complaint about the inclusive playground.

What the fuck was happening? Had the fire burned through common sense and integrity and the ties that bound my people together so thoroughly that we couldn't even agree that an inclusive playground for kids with mobility struggles, with cognitive and sensory challenges was a good thing?

But, no joke, there were three hundred signatures.

Three hundred.

In my town of ten thousand.

I was trying to do the math, trying to reassure myself that it was only three percent of the population, that ninety-seven percent hadn't signed on to fuck over local kids.

Only...the quad had less than a hundred signatures in a month's time.

The complaint about hosting the soccer tournament on Labor Day weekend had collected two hundred over several weeks.

And the playground had three hundred signatures. In less than ten days.

So, yeah, concern was a heavy rock in my belly, and—

My office door swung open.

No knock.

Just...swung right open.

"Dad?" I asked, glancing at my father standing in the doorway, his brows drawn and something akin to panic crossing his face. But then it was gone, and I was left wondering if I'd imagined it and—

"What the hell is going on?" he bellowed, storming into my office and slamming the door behind him.

Bluster.

Annoyance with me.

Well, *that* was something I was used to.

"Have you lost your head?" he stomped toward my desk, rounding it and towering over me in a way that was also something I was used to, same as the curl of disappointment, the inkling of thinking—of maybe *knowing*—I wasn't enough, wouldn't ever be enough.

For him.

For my mother.

That was okay.

I had others. I had the family I'd built. The man I loved and who loved me back. I had a niece who was like my sister. I had friends who had my back and who I could rely on.

I didn't need to seek acceptance from this man for who I would never be enough.

"Hi, Dad," I said. "It's nice to see you at"—my eyes flicked to the clock on my monitor top right corner—"9:17pm at night."

Storm clouds on his face.

Luckily for me, I'd weathered many a storm from this man and my worth was no longer tied to him *or* his blustering.

He scowled. "I knew you'd be working."

I waited to see if he'd expand on that.

He did—of course, he did. My dad always had an opinion on everything I did. "You've been spending so much time with *Joel*"—he spat the name—"that you'll have to pull many late nights to catch up."

"I've worked many late nights both before and after Joel." I pushed my chair back and stood up, leaning against the edge of my desk so my dad wouldn't tower over me quite so much. "That's not going to change now."

A huff.

"So," I asked, "why are you really here?"

Silence, long enough that I stifled a sigh and glanced back to my computer, wondering how long he was planning on being here, wondering if I could somehow steer us back toward the tentative peace we'd managed since Joel had dressed him down at dinner a little while back.

That was over, apparently.

Yay for me!

The joys of being the only disappointing child of parents who just couldn't see me for what I was.

He crossed his arms. "You shouldn't intervene with the school board."

I began gathering up my papers, deciding that since this conversation was happening, I would definitely be ready to wrap things up once it was done. Plus, if I left soon, I could work from the house. At least there I could watch the Rush replay from bed, covered in blankets that smelled like Joel and peck away on my laptop. Or I could work in my beautiful office my man had so thoughtfully designed for me. "Believe me, I didn't want to intervene with the board, but they asked me to sit in on the meeting and I was happy to listen to all sides." I tapped the stack of files on the desktop, ordering them so they'd fit in my bag. "That was enough for them to come to their own agreement."

Something I hoped would hold with the greenscape plan.

And the playground and the soccer tournament and the books at the library.

Something I didn't have hope would work for the water conservation measures—there were too many different pressures from the state and water district and the drought was complicating things.

But I could deal with one petition, one fire—no pun intended —at a time.

It was when they started risking needing two hands to count the problems that I got a bit...stressed.

"It's not that easy," my dad pointed out.

My father had been the mayor before me.

I knew he knew that.

I also knew it because I was the fucking mayor myself, was going on my second term, and I'd weathered shit he'd never so much as had to plan for.

But I was still mayor—and not running screaming for the hills, moving away and on and to a place where no one knew me— because I loved River's Bend. I loved the people. I loved the topography, the way the hills were green now and blooming and the river was rushing because the Sierra snowpack was beginning to melt. I loved the history—how we'd been an important part of the Gold Rush, a stopping point, a place to refuel and get supplies while searching for treasure. I loved how we became a place to settle when the flurry had died down, a quiet community that had banded together against the rest of the world.

That we were dealing with petty shit like playgrounds and library books...

Was a bit depressing.

More than a bit, maybe, when I felt like I lived and breathed for this job.

When I wasn't sure I really wanted it. Wasn't sure I'd ever really wanted it.

My dad had hit term limits, and he'd encouraged me to run—along with almost every other person I'd spoken to—and I'd won and I did a good job and now I'd been elected to a second term after having run uncontested and...

What did I really want?

Late nights. Long meetings. Thankless decisions. Mediating fights.

Listening to my father telling me I should do this job better?

I was suddenly exhausted, ready to be done with this conversation, and ready to be home and in bed and planning, actually *planning* like I hadn't had time to do of late, what with the petitions and Willow and Veronica and Bailey and Dessie and—

My father.

Standing in my office.

Telling me I wasn't doing a good enough job.

"I know it's not easy," I said as I turned away from him, shutting down my desktop—something I was awful about remembering, but was glad I remembered then. Because it gave me an excuse to look away, to compose myself, to get my shit together. "I'm one of the few people who live in town who understand as well as you do." I shoved my folders in my backpack, hitched it over my shoulders, slipped my feet into my shoes. "Now, I'm tired and I'm going home." I looked up at him, holding his eyes. "And you should too."

"BR—"

I moved to the door, held it open. "I love you," I told him. "You're my dad, and that won't change. But"—I braced, pressed on—"I'm tired of this dynamic between us. I'm not your employee, and I know that I'm not the kid you want, that I'll never be my brother—"

"Don't you mention him."

Sharp words.

Cutting words.

Slicing deep and...it was another thing that was familiar.

"I know I'm not him," I said quietly. "But I'd like to find a way for me to be *me* when I'm with you. And—"

He started moving toward me, expression unreadable.

Except for his eyes.

They were cold.

Another slice. Another day.

"And," I said, my voice still quiet, but my throat now thick with emotion. "I'd like for us to find a way to be more than former mayors when it's just us."

He stopped in front of me.

I held very still, waited.

Hoped.

Then he turned on his heel and disappeared down the hall.

And I was in my empty office. Alone. Again.

Only...this time I had somewhere to go home to.

So, I did.

TWENTY-TWO

JOEL

"So," Amy said the morning after I'd returned to town, "The easiest route, of course, would be to set up a meeting with Willow and hope she signs. The alternative is filing for a contested divorce, like I mentioned previously."

All of this would take months.

Or, likely, years.

Fuck. I was an idiot.

But Amy was looking at me expectantly, and I held out a hand to take the paperwork she passed over. "Thank you." A beat. "For taking the time and for doing it all so quickly."

Her hand found mine, squeezed lightly. "You don't need to thank me. I'm just doing my job." Half of her mouth curved. "Though, I won't turn down a cocktail once this is all behind us."

However long *that* would take.

And, yeah, maybe I hadn't made it much beyond my pity party for one, no matter how often Ry's words had ricocheted through my mind.

"You're on," I told her.

But I must not have sounded convincing because she squeezed my hand again. "We'll get through it either way, it's just a matter of time, yeah?"

"Yeah," I whispered.

She patted my hand again, opened her mouth, but then there was a knock at the door, her receptionist poking her head in and saying, "Sorry to interrupt, but your next client is here."

Amy glanced up. "Just ask them to wait a moment."

"No," I told her quickly. "I've got to get going, anyway." I grabbed the folders and pushed out of the chair. "Thanks again. I'll be in touch."

Then I was out of that office and heading to the parking lot, walking to my car, typing out a message to the woman I'd barely spoken to since she'd shown up on my doorstep.

Using a number I hadn't looked at since my Rosie told me she'd programmed it into my phone. Sending,

> Can you meet me? It's Joel.

Barely thirty seconds passed before she sent back.

> When?

My fingers moved across the screen.

> Today? I've got a game tomorrow.

Longer this time, but eventually she replied.

> I can meet you at the coffee shop downtown in an hour.

An hour. Fuck, could this possibly be this easy? Would she meet me and sign the papers and we could put this shit behind us? My pulse sped, hope blooming even as I tried to ignore it, to remind myself that it likely wouldn't be this simple, that five years hadn't passed only to be resolved with some paperwork and a meeting at a coffee shop.

But hope was a vicious thing.

It grew like the toughest of weeds and withered like the fragilest of flowers. It could be as strong as concrete and rebar and as weak as a dried leaf.

Appearing in tiny cracks. Hiding in shadows.

Persisting despite the roughest of conditions.

So, I couldn't beat it down or hold it back or...

I typed out a text.

> I'll see you there.

Only...

I didn't.

I *didn't* see her there, not in an hour, not for the hour afterward, the hour I'd sat at a table, sipping two cups of coffee like I was just enjoying the warm spring morning, the sunshine shining down and settling on my skin...while that hope shriveled up.

Blew away like dust on the wind.

Gone.

"Joel."

I glanced up, and for once, my Rosie wasn't the woman I wanted to see. Not her lush, curvy body, nor her bright blond curls. Nor...the worried look on her face as she stood on the outside of the gate enclosing the coffee shop's patio.

She disappeared inside, reappearing seconds later on the courtyard where I was sitting.

"Where's your coffee?" I asked, eyes searching the sidewalk like Willow might just appear and then all would be cool.

See? Even in those dark, tiny crevices, the plague that was hope continued to grow.

"I'll get some in a minute." She dragged a chair close, fixed me with a look. "Spill."

There was no point in hiding it, no point in pretending this was something it wasn't. "Willow was supposed to meet me here."

"Amy gave you the papers."

Not anger that I was meeting another woman or worry that I was betraying her. Billie had told me she'd committed to doing better, to having my back, and...she was just doing it.

Because that was my Rosie.

"Yeah." I held up the sheaf.

"And Willow was going to sign them?"

"I don't know," I sighed, wrenched myself out of my twisting mind. "I texted to meet, and she said she'd be here within the hour."

"So, clearly, *that* didn't happen."

The dry way she muttered that sentiment had me chuckling before I even realized I was laughing, had some of the knots in my stomach relaxing.

"No, it didn't."

"Hmm." Billie settled back in her chair. "I wonder if she knew what was coming."

"You think she heard about us going to Amy?"

A shrug. "It's a small town."

That was true. Gossip traveled through River's Bend at such a speed that Han Solo and his less-than-twelve-parsecs Kessel Run would be impressed.

"It's weird, though," Rosie murmured. "Holly told me that Willow had applied for a job at the home goods store, and she's been hanging around Monroe's, making friends." Billie tapped a finger along her bottom lip. "I just...she seems like she's getting settled, so I can't imagine that she would leave now."

Running again.

From me.

Fuck.

I bit back a sigh. "I don't know," I said, shifting closer, dragging her chair so it was almost pressed to mine, our legs tangled, her upper body near enough for me to bend and bury my face in her hair, inhaling that tart and sweet and *her*.

She leaned against me, hands on my waist. "I'll check with management at the apartment complex. See if she moved out or gave notice or..."

"Hey, Billie Rose!" a voice called, causing us to both turn around and watch as one of the young baristas pushed through the doors, carrying a mug. "Did you want a refill, Joel?" he asked after setting it on the table.

"Nah, thanks, Adam. I won't sleep tonight if I do."

Adam smiled and disappeared inside, but not before Billie had picked up the mug and started draining it like the professional coffee drinker she was.

"You okay?" she asked softly. "I know this didn't turn out as you probably hoped."

Hoped.

Fucking hell.

I pushed that away and nodded, then reached over and tugged at a curl. "Fine, sweetheart." Fake.

That sounded fucking fake.

"Drink up so we can go home," I said before she could dissect my tone too closely. "I think I have a kiss to punish you for."

But this was my Rosie. She'd heard my tone, and she didn't ignore it. Instead, she tilted her head to the side, curls bouncing, blue eyes seeing too much, and said softly, "You're okay. I'm okay. *We're* okay."

As long as *she* didn't run.

Like every other woman in my life had. Did. No, *had*—

Fuck.

Hello, intrusive thoughts.

And maybe it was just some of that Mayoral Magic or telepathy or just...*Billie Rose*. But whatever it was, she seemed to sense those persistent ideas pinging through my mind, and it had her coming closer, banding her arms around my middle and holding me tightly. "We're okay," she repeated.

I wanted to believe that.

I *did*.

I just...there was a heavy feeling in my stomach that wasn't feeling quite so optimistic.

It wasn't something I verbalized, though, not when it was twisted in my mind, tangled with the past and Willow and what Ryan had said, not when it was knotted with the present that Rosie and I were knee-deep in, the future I could almost taste.

So, instead, I shoved it down.

My woman needed me here. In the now. Not bogged down in emotions and the past and annoying, intrusive thoughts.

Breathe. Push through.

Good.

"We're okay," I agreed after a long moment.

And when, after I'd said that, she smiled up at me, I found myself relaxing, smiling back.

Believing.

We were okay.

We *had* to be.

TWENTY-THREE

BILLIE ROSE

I sighed and sat back in my chair, my head starting to ache.

It was Monday morning. Joel was on the road again—though thankfully, only for one game.

And my inbox was full.

Of complaints.

For and against the playground. Concern for "mature material" in the teen section of the library. The water guidelines from the state that would bankrupt local farmers. The greenscape plan that would harm property values and stifle the growth of the town. The Labor Day soccer tournament that would bring both too much traffic and not enough guests to justify the cost of hosting it.

Oh...and an independent investigator was conducting an audit of federal and state funds we'd received after the fire.

So. Much. Fun.

It was *so much fun* being the mayor.

I wasn't all that worried about the funding. If my dad had taught me nothing else, it was to follow protocol and play by the rules and document the shit out of everything. In triplicate.

Online, before and after our physical records were destroyed—making sure we always had a record, even when things went wrong. And I'd done the same in the aftermath of the fire.

But I couldn't lie.

Those days and weeks and months had been a bit of a blur—I couldn't be completely sure that I'd been perfect.

I could have made mistakes.

I could have—

"Crap," I muttered, rubbing my temples, knowing I was feeling on edge and out of control because I *couldn't* control the audit and because those days after the fire *had* been a blur. "I did the best I could with what I had. That will have to be enough."

Easy to say.

But...what if it wasn't?

I shoved up out of my chair and started pacing, thinking it through, knowing I was doing what I could, knowing I couldn't get more involved, even if I wanted to. I had to let the investigator run this, ask for what they needed, and give them the access they requested.

Such simple things.

Except for a control freak.

And, just for the record, *I* was the control freak.

A knock echoed through the door—at the perfect freaking time, thank God for interruptions while I was spiraling in my control freakness.

"Come in," I called, watching the door swing open, ready for that interruption from my thoughts.

Ready for *any* interruption.

Except Bella, my assistant, wasn't coming in with a surprise cup of coffee or an invitation to lunch, not if the grim expression on her face was any indication.

My lungs tightened. My spine went stiff.

"What is it?" I asked.

"There are some people here who want to talk to you," she

said. "I told them you were busy and asked if I could make an appointment, but—"

"I need to speak to the mayor *now,*" a woman said, pushing by Bella and barreling into my office, a handful of others coming in behind her.

I rocked back on my heels, surprised and my mind racing, trying to remember her name. She was one of the newer residents in town, but Maia, Bonnie, and Aubree were familiar faces, and knowing them, feeling the tension immediately ramp up, I knew that this mix of personalities would not bode well for me.

"It's good, Bella," I said. "Can you push my meeting with the controller? I'll call him at the end of the day, okay?"

Bella nodded, but the good assistant that she was, she left the door open.

A silent message.

Not leaving me alone.

I held that feeling close, knowing that this confrontation wasn't going to be fun, wasn't going to be something I wanted to tackle alone.

And yet, it was the mayor's job.

A throat cleared. Impatiently.

"How can I help you, ladies?" I asked, leaning on the edge of my desk.

"My daughter has been *corrupted!*" the new woman—Karen, sweet baby Jesus, her name was *Karen,* I remembered now—exclaimed, plunking her hands on her hips and scowling at me.

I waited, searched the other women's faces, expecting one of the four of them to, I don't know, *expand* on that statement? When they didn't, I took a breath and forced my tone to be neutral. "Could you speak a little further on why you think that is the case?"

Wide eyes. Pink flaring on her cheeks. Karen tossed her head, the short, blond strands of her hair dancing. She leaned toward me, fury in every syllable. "She's reading *filth!*"

The library then.

I struggled to keep my face neutral—amusement and annoyance were warring—but I did it. I kept my face straight and my tone even. "Why don't we go down the hall—"

"I will not be removed!" Karen snapped. "I will be heard and—"

"Where we all can sit down and talk about this?" I finished without missing a beat, without acknowledging her mid-outburst outburst. I glanced at Aubree, who I knew was soft and easily manipulated, but a good person overall, and inclined my head.

She bit her lip.

But I'd done my part.

I pushed off the desk, moved to the door, and turned down the hall.

And...thankfully, they followed me to the conference room, though Karen was still sputtering.

"In here, ladies," I said, opening the door and connecting eyes with Bella. "I'm good," I mouthed. Then I stifled another sigh, walked into the room, and prepared to meet my fate.

Filthy reading material was apparently on this mayor's agenda for the day.

Joy of joys.

———

It wasn't joyful.

It wasn't anywhere near that emotion.

It wasn't anywhere near positive.

And if my head had been starting to ache before, it was positively throbbing now, a raging headache that was turning the edges of my vision blurry, making my neck and shoulders and hell, my whole body feel like I'd run a goddamned marathon.

"Christ," I muttered, not sure if I'd made the situation with Karen, Aubree, Bonnie, and Maia any better.

Or if I'd wake up and my inbox would be flooded with more complaints and a petition with hundreds more signatures.

Or the library books—its *filth*—hauled from the shelves and burned to ashes in the parking lot.

The worst part of it? Karen's daughter was seventeen.

Was only three months away from *eighteen*.

And her mom was worried about a few dirty books.

Groaning, I thumped my head on my desk and thought of the call I'd just had to make to the head librarian, warning her that the shitstorm didn't stop with the petition, but that parents—and no pun intended—*Karens* were involved and getting louder.

An inventory of the teen catalogue was where we were starting, identifying books that might have mature themes.

But I had no clue if that would be enough, or if we'd need to create a rating system and go further—requiring parent permission and under eighteens not able to check those "mature" books out without their parents signing off on it. I hated all of this, from the mature themes to the idea of a parent giving kids who were old enough to make choices about what they wanted to read permission to do so.

This wasn't a kindergartner reading romance novels.

It was a young woman choosing how she spent her spare time, and I didn't want to stifle that exploration or the urge to learn or stomp on her enjoyment of something like reading, which was so important.

So, I was uncomfortable and unsure of the right way forward and—

Tired.

Of River's Bend.

My cell rang, and—no joke—I almost let the call go, but when I flipped it over, saw it was Joel, the hardness of the day disappeared.

"Hey, honey," I said after swiping and putting it up to my ear.

"Hey, Rosie baby."

I blinked. Froze.

Because he sounded relaxed and happy, and it had been weeks now since I'd heard him like that—not since Willow had shown up.

"Your day good?" he asked.

I wasn't about to shit on this happy and relaxed man. "Yeah," I said, "it was fine."

"Good, sweetheart." A beat. "My parents called, and they want to come up for the weekend. Would that be okay? My sisters can all make it, and this time they wanted to bring their kiddos and spouses, and since one of our last home games of the season is on Saturday, it'll be a Marshall family reunion."

Joel was happy.

Relaxed.

Excited.

So, how could I do anything other than shove away my shitty day and focus on that, on him, on the fact that his family was nice and it would be good to see them again, despite everything else going on?

How could I say anything but, "sounds like a plan"?

Newsflash, I couldn't.

And now, apparently, I had a family reunion to plan.

Twenty-Four

JOEL

"Get me, Uncle Joel!" my niece, Emma, said. "Get me!"

I growled, took one step in her direction, and she hauled ass, shrieking as she went. I turned back to my Rosie. "Apparently, I've got to *get* her."

Billie smiled up at me, a wineglass in her hand only because I'd managed to wrestle her away from the kitchen and her prep of seventeen—a slight exaggeration, but it was a lot of them—charcuterie boards.

She had fruit and cheese with jam and honey, meat and cheese with crackers, butter and bread with a shit ton of toppings, a brownie and cookie board with frosting and candy and sprinkles (and was probably why I was ten seconds away from chasing my niece across my back yard). And I'd pulled her away from making her "dessert one."

My niece and nephews didn't need more sugar.

The adults didn't need more food.

But I got it. The last time she'd met my family, she'd been

smack dab in the middle of Mayor Duties. She'd arrived late and flustered and...

Today was her chance to make up for that.

Calm and collected and showing off her Billie Rose magic.

My parents and sisters had liked her before, but today, they got it. The warmth of my Rosie, the way she was comfortable in her own skin and managed to make each and every person, from my seven-year-old niece, Emma, to my two-year-old nephew, James, to my mom and sisters and dad, feel welcome and included was on full display.

But...I wanted her to feel like she didn't need to be on display.

That she could just be.

Here. Now. Not trying to make up for something, not putting on that magic.

Because the magic was there without her frantically dusting corners and making charcuterie boards and rearranging six vases of flowers a half dozen times.

Because the magic was Billie herself.

But...

I looked closer for the first time since I'd pulled into the driveway, car full of suitcases and kids, my parents and siblings and their spouses in the rentals behind me, Billie greeting us on the porch with bubbles for the kids and glasses of wine for my sisters and mom, beers for my dad and me and brothers-in-law. "You okay, Rosie baby?"

She blinked, focused on me. "Sorry, what?"

I brushed my knuckles over her cheek. "Sweetheart."

"Joel," she whispered—and there it was again, that flash of a shadow, of something that sent my instincts prickling.

"Hey—" I began, hand on her jaw, drawing her closer.

"Uncle Joel!" Emma screeched.

An exhalation, her smile coming back, the blip I'd seen in her eyes disappearing. "You've got to go *get* her."

"Billie."

Her hand came to mine, gently peeling it away from her skin, turning it, and pressing a kiss to my palm. "*Get* her, honey," she ordered softly. "This isn't super important. I promise it will hold."

I crouched a little so I could meet her eyes, relieved when she didn't try to look away, when she didn't hide from me. "You sure?"

"Yes." She held up her wine. "This is all I need right now."

"And this," I told her, snagging the remains of the cheeseboard —and the paltry piece of brie that was left—and putting it in front of her.

"Fuck," she whispered.

"What?" I whispered back.

"I love you."

My lungs inflated in a rush. "I—"

"*Uncle! Joel!*"

"Go," she ordered, mouth curved. "I've got my cheese."

I laughed, kissed the top of her head, and then I rushed off...

To *get* my niece.

Which, of course, ended up with my nephew chasing us on his chubby little legs, roaring at us in a high-pitched pterodactyl screech, hands up and fingers bent like claws.

"You're a T-Rex, Uncle Joel!"

I scooped up James, tossing him onto my shoulder. "Then you'd better *run*, little stegosaurus!"

———

"I have to admit," my mom said later that night. "I was concerned."

I frowned, dropping my beer away from my mouth and setting it on the railing of the deck. "About what?"

Silence that had me turning slowly to face her.

"Concerned about what?" I pressed.

"Billie."

Instantly, my blood pressure began to rise. "Mom."

Her hand covered mine. "She was...well, I won't lie to you. She didn't make the best impression the last time we came, and I know that people deserve grace and are allowed to have bad days, but I was worried, honey." Her voice dropped. "I didn't want you to end up with another Willow."

I froze. She didn't know what was going on with my ex, didn't know that Willow was back in town, didn't know about the non-divorce or my idiocy for not following up on it.

I'd tell them.

I just...wanted this weekend without my fuck up shadowing every moment.

"You deserve someone who will be there for you as much as you're there for her," my mom murmured.

"Billie's—"

A squeeze. "I know, baby. I saw that today. I *see* it"—she waved a hand out to where Billie was lying on a pile of blankets in the yard, staring up at the sky with my niblings, their excited chatter reaching my ears—"now. I get it, so no need to be upset and protective on her behalf."

My mom smiled when I managed to tear my eyes away.

"She hides it," I told her. "She didn't have this. Not what we have."

"That's a shame." A cluck of her tongue. "I was concerned because I wanted my baby boy to have someone who'd look after him like you look after the people you love. Because you deserve to have that."

My throat tightened.

Ryan.

Now my mom.

"I know that, Mom," I murmured, looking back out at Rosie, at my sisters and niece and nephew, feeling that settle deep in my middle.

"Do you?"

I was...getting there.

But I didn't want to talk about it, not right then, not this weekend.

Not as I was still wrestling with the logic of that and the fact that my past had taught me differently, even though I'd never really fucking thought about it that way, not until it was thrown smack dab in my face, forcing me to confront it.

Confront why it had hurt when Billie had left me.

Confront the nagging insecurity of Willow and the others doing the same.

There was something wrong with me—but...what if there wasn't?

No. There *wasn't*.

I sighed, nodded. "I'm working on it."

Quiet—between us—because the night itself wasn't quiet. It was punctuated with conversations and exclamations and giggles from my sisters and Billie and James and Emma, all overseen by my dad observing from my deck chair, sipping his beer, my brothers-in-law clustered around him.

My mom rested her head on my shoulder. "That's all we can ask, honey."

I didn't have a reply to that—and maybe one wasn't necessary, anyway. Maybe it was enough to be here, with the people I loved, and to be working on it.

So, I wrapped my arm around her and held her close and...

I worked on it.

I thought about why these feelings were so strong, why they'd hit now, why they mattered enough that they kept digging their claws into my mind, and I knew it was because Billie mattered, because what we were building together *mattered*.

Because I had won her over.

Because I was waiting for her to leave me.

Because...that was what always happened.

But that didn't have to be my future, so I held my mom and

watched my Rosie, and I stood there under the night sky and had a fucking epiphany.

I was worried she would leave me because all the women I'd been with had and because she was a woman who I felt more for than any of the others. My heart had been carved out of my chest and served up on a silver platter for her.

She *owned* me.

So, yeah, of course I was worried.

Because I didn't know how to make sure she didn't leave me.

TWENTY-FIVE

BILLIE ROSE

I padded across the kitchen, the tiles cool on my bare feet, and debated.

Between polishing off the cookie butter board—snicker-doodles, *drool*—and pouring another glass of wine.

Then I thought about the week...and decided to have both.

I'd earned it on Monday with the library books, and Tuesday with the greenscape and my normal mayoral duties. Wednesday was a council meeting, and it was one that ran longer than any previously because there were a lot of residents attending...and a lot of complaints to be made. Thursday had been lost to soccer planning—the fields needed to be reserved—and a long call with the executive board for the library. And yesterday, I'd made my rounds downtown, had grocery shopped, cleaned the house from top to bottom, and slapped shit on wooden boards.

And by slapped, I meant I spent hours carefully arranging each slice of fruit and cheese and meat...and sprinkle and spread of butter and—

I'd gone overboard.

But I'd just wanted everything to be perfect.

Luckily, it had gone great—not perfect, because nothing ever did and I'd ended up with more than one smear of butter and frosting on my clothes and the cabinets...and the new couch.

That was all fixable, though.

I hadn't been late or had a meltdown, and everyone's belly had been happy.

Totally winning at life.

Not *work* life, but personal life, and that was a victory I was going to take.

So, wine *and* snickerdoodles and taking my planner out onto the porch for some playtime with my stickers. Humming to myself, I got my cookies, my wine, and tiptoed down the hall to retrieve my planner bag, then tiptoed back through the kitchen and to the French doors that led to the back yard, hand going to the handle—

"You might want to put some socks on first, sweetheart."

I squeaked, jumping so high I nearly dropped the glass of wine I'd just poured, so fully lost in my thought of booze and sugar and stickers and washi, I apparently hadn't registered Rob, Joel's dad, at the counter, his glasses perched on the edge of his nose, his cell's screen on full brightness.

How had I missed that?

And him?

And...

I blew out a breath, set my—thankfully unspilled—wine glass down and turned to smile at Rob. "Sorry," I said, heart still pounding, "I didn't see you there."

"No kidding." But the words were gentle, and his smile was soft.

And that was weird. I wasn't used to men his age being soft, not with me, and it wasn't just my dad. It was...all of them. I was their boss or a competitor or someone annoying who made them do shit they didn't want to do.

No, that wasn't fair.

Some of the older guys interacted nicely with me—like they would pat a puppy on the head or ruffle a little boy's hair.

I just...well, the nice ones never really stood out, did they?

People always remembered the bad ones.

"Can I get you anything?" I asked, after what was probably a rude-as-hell pause.

He took off his glasses, set them on the counter. "You want to take a load off? Or do you really have the night air in mind?"

That wasn't getting him something, and as such, my brain short-circuited. "Um..." was the only thing I could manage.

"Right." He stood up, leaving his glasses and phone on the counter. "You want the night air." He tugged open the door, smiling back at me. "I can't blame you. There's something about the way River's Bend smells that always settles me."

Mutely, I walked toward the open door, stepped out when he swept his hand toward the deck.

"Though," he went on, following me out, "it's the sky that really gets me. We're in California, not that far from Sacramento, and somehow the stars are out like we're in the middle of the wilderness."

"It's the foothills of the Sierras," I was able to force out. "Lots of green space and animals and"—a bit of the mayor took over—"we're lucky to be both close to and sheltered from the large thoroughfares that lead up to Tahoe."

"Quiet convenience."

My lips curved, and I sat down, putting my glass and cookie on the table, my planner bag next to them. "I might have to use that for the next tourism campaign."

He chuckled, settled into his own chair with a sigh.

And...silence.

I reached for my wine glass, froze. "Are you sure I can't get you anything?"

His head turned, and under the darkness, the peace and quiet and shadows of the night, I was struck by how much he looked like Joel.

And struck by the urge for my man to turn silver fox.

"If you want quiet and I'm intruding on that," Rob said, "I can go inside."

My gut sank. "N-no," I stammered. "Th-that's not what I meant at all. I'm out here with my wine and my cookie—I can at least get you a beer and something to eat and—"

"Rosie," he said on a sigh, leaning close enough that he could pat my hand. "Do you want to be alone?"

"No," I whispered.

"Okay." He sat back, crossed his ankles, one over the other. "Then I'm going to sit here while you enjoy your snack—because no, Rosie girl, you can't get me anything else, otherwise my stomach is going to explode."

"I—" I bit my lip. "Okay."

It took a minute for me to settle in, to relax enough so I could sip my wine and eat my cookie, but eventually I *did* relax as we sat silently, managing to not ask him if he was sure, *really* sure I couldn't get him anything. Unfortunately, I was totally unable to summon any Mayoral Magic to make small talk.

Rob didn't appear to have that problem. "Joel doesn't share a lot."

My glass was empty, but I suddenly had the urge to go inside and refill it. "He likes to take care of things himself." I laughed softly, turned to Rob, and smiled self-deprecatingly. "Kind of like me." A shrug. "I'm guessing that's why we struggled to get along at first." Another. "And why we get along now."

"I'm guessing that's true," Rob said, chuckling to himself. But then his expression and tone grew serious, and my stomach began churning.

This was the point where disappointment would be expressed.

And I didn't *want* it to be expressed.

I wanted them to like me, to want me, to include me, to love—

"But he talked about you."

I inhaled so sharply I nearly choked on my own spit. Okay, fine. I *did* choke on my own spit, coughing as I tried to get my lungs and throat to chill before I upchucked wine and cookie everywhere.

Rob's hand found mine again. "That tells me enough."

"The choking on my own spit?" I wheezed.

"That my boy loves you," he replied softly.

Another rapid inhalation, though this time—thankfully—I didn't choke.

Rob squeezed my hand. "That was enough for me. He loves you. He's happy and settled in a way I've never seen before. But, Rosie, today I got to know *you*."

My eyes started to burn.

"I got to see how much you care—for him, for us because we matter to him, and that's more than enough for me, sweetheart. *More* than enough."

"Rob," I croaked. "I love him too."

"I know that." His mouth turned up. "So, breathe and know we're good. No need to work your ass off to get on my good side. No need to worry that I don't like you. You're good for my son and you love him, and that's enough." He sat back. "Put aside everything else for a little bit and look after yourself. Drink the wine and eat the cookies and open up that bag you made a special trip to retrieve. I'm just an old man who's content to sit across from a nice woman his son is crazy about while we both enjoy the night sky and fresh air."

I didn't know what to do with that.

Okay, I *did* know what to do with that—because it was similar to what I shared with Joel, how he helped me settle in my own skin. It just wasn't fatherly, or what I'd come to know was fatherly and—

My dad wasn't Rob.

There.

That was the truth, and it hurt to accept that, to know I wouldn't ever have what Joel did.

But...I could have this.

Quiet and night air and stars overhead and a man who was content to sit beside me, just because I loved his son.

"Yeah?" he asked softly.

"Yeah," I agreed.

And then I pulled out my planner, and I got to work.

Not surprisingly, I had to educate him on the various uses for washi tape.

Twenty-Six

Joel

Cold on my cheeks.

Fans in the stands.

My skates crunching on the ice. Pucks flew. My teammates stretched and moved by me, each completing their own intricately crafted warm-up.

Created sometimes by a coach. Other times by a trainer.

But mostly formed from years and years of superstition.

Or maybe that was just mine—my routine starting with a nap and then getting to the rink early, eating the same three combinations of foods several hours before—pasta, chicken, broccoli. Salt, pepper, olive oil, a dash of cayenne (because I needed it to taste like *something* and the salt, pepper, and just olive oil weren't doing it).

Sleep. Food. Not rushing to the rink.

Because once I strode through the doors of the arena, everything moved at warp speed. It was finding a way to warm up off the ice first, to loosen the muscles and get my head ready to play. A stationary bike was my preferred method, but it was preferred by a lot of the other guys too, so there wasn't always enough time to get on one. If the bikes were too crowded, I ended up jogging up and down the halls, getting my heart rate up and my body moving.

Then it was soccer, a group of us juggling a ball back and forth, tuning up those reflexes.

After that, stretching.

Only then did I get dressed, in left side, right side order.

Socks and jock and shin guards and then *hockey* socks, pants, skates. A pause to fuss with my laces. Tape to keep my shin guards in place.

Upper body—shoulder and elbow pads, sweater (hockey jersey), helmet, and gloves, my mouth guard tucked safely into a crevice of one of the latter.

If I had to tape my stick, that fell between lower and upper body.

Because after, it was more stretching.

Finally, I drank a mix of electrolytes and water and a dash of protein, which tasted like shit, but ever since I'd gotten a hat trick when I was twenty-two, I'd kept up with the practice.

It kept my legs moving and my mind focused.

Or maybe it was all bullshit.

Either way, it had become part of my routine and I was too damned old to change it at this point in my career.

But now I'd progressed past getting dressed and drinking my magic water, and I'd hopped out onto the ice with the rest of the guys. Since it was well before game time—there would be the warm-up and then an ice cut, the national anthem and *then* the puck would drop—the stands weren't all that full, but I heard, "Uncle Joel!" as I skated by our bench.

Grinning, I looked across the ice, saw Emma decked out in a Rush jersey, my number painted on her cheeks, her chubby arm waving.

Fuck, I wanted one of those.

I wondered if I could convince Billie to create our future in reverse order.

Because for the first time ever, I wanted a kid of my own.

A little girl with curls and blue eyes. A little hellion with green irises that matched mine and a messy mop of hair I'd love to tousle—

"Go, Uncle Joel!" Emma shouted as I reached the glass and grinned at her.

"Ready, peanut?" I called, scooping up a puck.

She plunked her hands onto her hips. "I'm *not* a peanut."

"She's got you there," Fox said, skating up behind me and waving one of his giant paws at my niece. "Hi, princess!" he called.

"I'm not a *princess* either," Emma retorted.

Fox tilted his head to the side and called again, "What are you?"

She lifted both of her arms in the air, fists tight. "I'm a hockey fan!" she yelled.

Fox's expression was comical then he grinned wide. "That's my girl!"

Emma scowled. "I'm Uncle Joel's girl!"

I was laughing now, so hard that I could barely keep myself upright on my skates, and my family wasn't any better, my mom and dad, sisters and brother-in-laws busting up. My Rosie was holding Emma up so my niece could better see over the boards, so she was slightly more composed. But only slightly, because she was laughing, her smile warming me straight through.

She was just multitasking—making sure that my niece didn't face plant into the glass *while* laughing at me.

I loved her.

So fucking much.

So much that I found myself placing my hand on the glass, my heart skipping a beat when she freed up one of hers and lined it up with mine.

I wasn't even touching her, and my pulse felt like it was raging through me like a runaway locomotive, like I'd gotten caught out on the ice and was now having to haul ass back into our own zone.

"Unc-y Joe-y!"

My gaze shot to the left, to James, hopping up and down in my sister, Kira's, lap.

"Hoo-ky fan!" His arms jiggled as he copied his sister, screaming like the little maniac he was.

Fox grinned. "Kids are the best, man."

"Whatever you say, *princess*," Ry said, scooping up a puck and tossing it over the glass so my dad could catch it and pass it over to James.

I tossed mine to Rosie, and she handed it to Emma, and then, because there was suddenly a swarm of kids at the glass, we repeated the process until everyone who wanted one had a puck.

With no further reason to delay, I waved and followed Ry and Fox away from the boards.

Then I went through the rest of my routine—six wrist shots, one in each corner, the other two in random spots I rotated. Sometimes a foot off the ground to either side, sometimes at a bad angle, sometimes five-hole (between the goalie's legs). After shooting time, I moved on to stick handling to warm up my wrists and shoulders. Then a few skating drills to feel my blades beneath me.

And finally, perhaps my most favorite of pastimes during warm-ups, it was time for shit-talking.

Leaning on the top of the bench with Fox and Ry at my sides, giving them a hard time (along with any of my teammates who happened to skate by). Laying it on extra thick to the other team, picking on the rookies, jibing at the old guys (like me) who might have a loose hold on their temper (*not* like me—I was steady and sneaky at revenge and didn't often drop my gloves).

It was both the least and most important part of getting my head into the game.

Because it was unnecessary and totally needed.

Obviously, I didn't need to chirp, but giving each other shit was a surefire way to release the pregame tension.

Bonus was that it sometimes messed with the other team's mojo.

Not often.

But, that night, a few guys on the other side of the red line stumbled or missed shots and I liked to think it was because of Ry, Fox, and I.

Whatever I had to tell myself, right?

Regardless, time ticked down on the jumbotron overhead and the guys began leaving the ice and heading to the locker rooms— the last push and prep before game time. I stayed till the buzzer went, though, stayed until my team was completely off the ice.

Before I hopped off and headed down the hall, I glanced back across at my family, who waved and pounded the glass and generally went nuts.

Because they were here to support me.

Because they were willing to put the effort in.

Because they'd never left.

Something settled inside me as my gaze drifted to the left, to the woman who was smiling but not banging on the glass.

Only because her arms were full of niblings.

I blew Billie a kiss, laughed when she jerked her head back like it had actually struck home, making James and Emma toss their heads back, their giggles in the air.

Yeah, I needed to make some of those.

And I knew it was because of the woman standing there— smile wide and arms full.

Because, win or lose, I knew she would be there for me.

Always.

TWENTY-SEVEN

BILLIE ROSE

I was sitting next to the city controller, the financial services manager, and the finance committee members.

And a pit was growing in my stomach by the second.

Because sitting across from me was Phoebe Connors.

The typical elementary and middle and high school mean girl.

My bully.

From kindergarten through senior year. She'd hated everything about me—my clothes, my hair, my pasty ass skin. My laugh. The fact that I always was on the Honor Roll and never missed a soccer game.

She'd moved away for college.

And now—apparently— she was back.

As the lead auditor who was going to go through every bit of paperwork from the last five years. With—her words—"a special focus on how the finances were handled after the fire."

The universe hated me.

It knew I was exasperated with the town and the petitions and the job, and it had handed me the biggest challenge of the position to date.

In the form of Phoebe Connors.

Who was just as beautiful, just as tall and skinny and perfectly coiffed.

She even looked good under the harsh fluorescent lighting they put in every freaking government building.

Well, know what?

I looked good.

Joel's family had gone home two days before, his sisters and their hubbies needing to return to work. And that morning, I'd gotten not one, but two orgasms before Joel left on the bus at the crack of dawn.

He'd been riding a high after scoring twice in the game on Saturday night, and now they were wrapping up their last couple of away games. They'd have one more home and one more away game when he returned. And then...playoffs.

It was crunch time.

So naturally, I'd laid a kiss on him that had made him all growly.

And so *I'd* promised to be naked and waiting for him on Thursday when he got home so he could "punish me."

I couldn't wait.

Plus, I'd finally figured out how to make my winged liner not look splotchy.

Thanks, TikTok.

But, even with that newfound confidence, I wasn't sure I was going to come out on top in this.

Phoebe looked...positively gleeful.

An expression I'd seen on many occasions over the years, had seen often enough to know the pit in my stomach, the one that existed beneath the crevice Joel had filled in over the last few weeks, was likely the proper indicator of how the interaction was going to go.

I glanced at my watch, eager to rip off the Band-Aid and get this shit over with. "Should we get started? Or..."

"I'm just waiting for my assistant," Phoebe said haughtily, stacking papers and barely bothering to look up at me as she spoke.

The controller sighed, but I didn't bother to acknowledge Phoebe's slight.

I knew how to play this game.

And what I'd learned from kindergarten all the way up to senior year was that engaging or getting mad or trying to get the better of Phoebe never worked. It was much better to mind my p's and q's, to keep my head down and press on.

Which was something I was fully on board with.

Until Phoebe's assistant walked in.

She was tall and thin and had that contour down. The winged liner and beautiful body and poreless complexion.

Willow.

Willow was Phoebe's fucking assistant.

———

I picked up my cell, and I tried to stop my hands from shaking as I typed out a text to Joel.

> I need to talk to you.

But just as I went to hit send, my eyes landed on the clock, and I registered the time.

He would be right in the middle of his pregame routine, maybe finishing up his nap if the bus had been delayed, and if not, he'd be finishing his ride on the stationary bike. Did I really want to interrupt him with this shit?

Shit he couldn't deal with three hundred miles away from River's Bend.

Shit that wasn't really anything because nothing abnormal had happened during the meeting after Willow had walked in.

Except for the fact that she *had* walked in.

And sat beside Phoebe as though she didn't know me, as though I wasn't with her freaking husband or hadn't set her up in an apartment, as though she hadn't applied for a job at Holly's.

As though, *I* hadn't shared my fucking cheese with her and thrown her a welcome party, (however passive-aggressive it was) and—

I set my cell down on my desk and stared at the screen.

For a long fucking time.

Long enough for my hands to stop shaking and the churning in my stomach to settle and for my mind to clear.

I reached out and began tapping, began hitting the backspace button—*tap, tap, tap*—not stopping until the message was gone, until the screen was clear of words that would make him worry when he needed to focus, words that could hold because nothing would be decided today, nothing would change the fact that Willow and Phoebe were working together and all of this weird shit with Willow showing up in River's Bend was probably connected with the audit and—

"Breathe," I whispered.

This could wait. We'd given the requested access, clarified some questions on the financial tracking system—or at least the supervisor on the financial committee had.

There was nothing to do but sit back and wait for Phoebe— and apparently *Willow*—to do their jobs.

Only, I couldn't help the sinking sensation, that pit in my stomach growing larger and faster than the crevice ever had. That it was too much of a coincidence with Willow and the audit and the petitions and...

Fucking *Phoebe Connors.*

Maybe I was being ridiculous in somehow feeling like this was about me, or about me and Joel. Maybe I was as bad as Phoebe, thinking the world revolved around me—and *only me, dammit!* Maybe this was just a series of shit that life threw at people, a typical craptastic slap from the universe reminding me that living on this planet was far from easy.

"Just breathe and think, Rosie," I whispered, channeling Joel and his calming presence and how he saw through my shields in a way no one else ever had, and...just thinking about him—and breathing—had my pulse slowing, my body relaxing.

I swiped up on the message app, closing it and my text chain with Joel.

He'd be home in two days.

We'd talk about it then, and maybe I'd call Amy in the morning and set up a meeting, just so we could game plan with someone.

One plus of Willow being Phoebe's assistant in the audit was that she was here in town.

Maybe Joel could sweet talk her into signing the papers, into shoving one of those pieces of shit the universe had handed to us on a platter into the trash.

Maybe this would be a good thing.

"Right," I whispered out loud, looking around my empty office as though someone might magically appear to answer (and agree with) me—and seriously, I might joke about Mayoral Magic, but unfortunately, my powers did not include teleportation.

"Sad," I muttered, feeling mildly better because I had the barest bones of a plan as I shut down my computer, packed up my stuff, and shook my head at my ridiculous wishes for Mayoral Magic.

Seriously, teleportation would be *cool.*

Distraction was *also* cool—and effective enough that I was able to make it out of the building without collapsing into a rocking, sweating ball of panic.

Especially when Dessie called and invited me to Monroe's for drinks.

More distraction.

More focus on things I could control—namely how to best go about demolishing a bottle of my favorite white from Napa Valley.

But the distraction didn't last long.

Because midway through my second glass, Willow walked in with Phoebe.

That distraction poofed away, the worry came back, the pit deepened.

Because I knew—*knew*—this shit had all just gotten infinitely more complicated.

TWENTY-EIGHT

JOEL

My body ached, and I had a bruise the size of a fucking watermelon blooming on my ribs.

But I was still hustling my ass up the stairs.

Because my Rosie had texted me a couple of hours ago saying quote, "I'm ready for my punishment."

So, tired legs, a long season almost behind me with only two games left, and the playoffs ahead (though hopefully they would be long as well...long enough to lead to the Calder Cup)—none of that mattered. I was home, my woman was waiting for me, and I'd had three-plus hours to get creative. To *plan*.

I grinned, was practically rubbing my hands together as I made it to the open bedroom door, and—

My feet stuttered.

"Hi," she whispered.

Fuck. Fuck. *Fuck.*

I had plans.

I'd spent time getting creative.

And my Rosie was standing in front of me, high heels on her

feet, naked except for a necklace...that wasn't really a necklace. It had a thick leather strap that was wrapped around her throat and silver chains that were connected to it and draping down and—

My dick went hard.

The links jingled as she moved, spinning slowly in a circle, the curves of the sparkling silver chains shifting, giving me glimpses of taut pink nipples, but only for a second because she was still turning and...*that ass*.

"Fuck," I growled.

She grinned at me over her shoulder, a smirk that had my cock aching, every sore and tired muscle and body part magically healed.

I could fuck this woman for an eternity.

Could lick and suck and bite—

"You like it?" she whispered, finishing the circle, those chains dancing on her skin.

I strode over to her, fingertips brushing the links of metal. "Why don't you have any panties on?"

A wicked grin, her body drifting closer. "How are you going to punish me if I do?"

"I should make you put them on." I gripped her hips, drew her closer. "That would be a bigger punishment."

She smirked, lifting up on tiptoe because even with her heels, she still had to stretch up to press her mouth to mine. Which she did. For a second. Because then her teeth were sinking into my bottom lip, nipping sharply, sending a bolt of pain through me.

Pain. Then need. Then *pleasure*.

I growled.

She dropped back on her heels, turned away again, one leg lifting, as though she was going to crawl onto the bed.

I slid my hand around to her front and gripped the metal links, the cool pieces biting into my skin, but I didn't yank her back against me like I wanted, like the red tinging the edges of my vision demanded. I used the chains to hold her in place, one leg up, that glistening pussy on display.

"Hands on the bed," I ordered.

Her breath caught, but she bent at the waist, palms dropping to the blankets.

"This ass," I groaned, running my hand over the curves, sliding my finger along that tight pucker, hovering there until she arched, trying to get me to increase the pressure.

"It's yours."

"I know." I tugged at those chains, dragging them over her nipples, using them to bend her further.

"Joel!"

Because I'd slipped a finger into that tight, wet pussy.

"You want more?"

She gasped, bucked against me.

"You want more," I murmured, leaning over her, my free hand plucking at her nipples, rolling them between thumb and forefinger, her moan the best sound in the world, her body pressing back against mine the best sensation.

I slid another finger in.

Her pussy clamped tight.

"More?"

"*Joel.*"

"More," I said against her skin.

I thrust faster, harder, but I didn't give her what she so clearly wanted. That was her punishment—and mine—for the kiss and the teasing, the chains and this glorious body. "This hot fucking cunt."

She rode my fingers, head falling back against my shoulder.

Moans on her tongue. My name in the air.

Her pussy clamping tight, rhythmically, and I knew she was close.

So, I pulled my fingers free.

"Joel!" she screamed, bucking against me, as though her hips were moving on their own, trying to get my fingers back, trying to convince them to keep stroking.

I licked my fingers cleaned, and—*fuck*—that was good. "You're being punished, remember?" My dick was pushing against my zipper, and I wanted nothing more than to unbutton and unzip, to thrust home.

She started to turn, to put that leg down.

"Uh-uh." I tsked, holding her steady, and—*fuck*—the evidence of her desire, of her need, of her wetness glistening at the tops of her thighs, shining in the lights of the bedroom nearly undid me. I dropped to my knees, ran my tongue up one thigh, down the other, lapping her up, the sweet and tart of her like fucking ambrosia on my tongue.

"Joel"—her hips were pulsing, shifting, searching out my mouth—"please, honey, I just—"

"Up," I ordered, lifting her, setting her on the edge of the bed on her knees. "Christ," I muttered, taking in the sight of her, my vision hazed, my patience unraveling by the second.

Which was the moment that Billie Rose proved she was perfect for me.

Because she lost *hers*.

Rolling over on the bed, legs splayed, chains spreading, skin flashing, pussy on display.

And when I got close, ensnared by the sight of her, she hooked a leg around me and hauled me down over her. "I've been punished enough," she murmured, hands going to my shirt, yanking it up.

Fuck.

It was tempting, so fucking tempting, to let her take over, to drive us both to a quick and pleasurable end.

I'd enjoy myself.

She would too.

But that wasn't what I wanted, wasn't what I'd planned, wasn't what I'd spent those hours on the bus putting my creative energy into.

Smirking, I unhooked her foot, pressing a kiss to her ankle

before unbuckling that sexy, high heel, allowing it to fall to the floor. "Nice try, Rosie baby." I nipped at her calf, the inside of her knee, her thigh with the glimmering wetness. A long, slow lick of my tongue through the slick folds of her pussy. "But I don't think you've been punished nearly enough."

I ran my hand through those chains then dragged it down, pressed my thumb to her clit. "You really put this on?" I asked as I stroked. "Knowing you had a punishment coming?"

"Joel," she murmured and her head was restless, rolling back and forth on the duvet.

Her thighs spread wider.

Those chains rattled.

I was nowhere in the realm of even pretending to be in control.

And it was fucking glorious.

Twenty-Nine

BILLIE ROSE

The chains were a mistake.

But also...not.

The way they rubbed against my skin, teased my nipples, some of the links warmed by my flesh, by his hands, the rest of them cold enough to make me shiver, to raise goose bumps all along my body was insane. As in, *I* was going insane. Or maybe that was because Joel had taken off my other heel, allowing it to drop to the floor with a thud that I barely heard. Because he was on his knees between my legs, slowly kissing his way up to my pussy again.

And stopping before getting to the good part, before getting his mouth on me, the hot puff of his breath as he hovered a millimeter from the motherland, the worst sort of tease.

Or maybe the best.

Or maybe—

Hell, I didn't know what the fuck I was thinking or feeling or—

A long, slow flick of his tongue.

I screamed, hips bucking, hands reaching down and swiping at his hair, intending to yank him against me, to ride his mouth until this pressure building inside me exploded.

Only, he was a hockey player. He was quick, quicker than me, jerking out of my reach, making it so my fingers only just brushed his hair, but couldn't capture it, couldn't lace my fingers in the thick blond strands, couldn't draw him to me and—

A nip to my inner thigh.

"Behave."

And just because I was me and that was an order and again, *I was me*, I looked down my body, beyond the parted chains draped over my torso, the hard buds of my nipples peeking through the strands of silver, down past my naked pussy, down to my parted legs and the man who was crouched between them, sucking lightly on the spot he'd bit, sending pulses of desire through me.

I was trembling and restless and—

I still fixed him with a glare. "No."

The smile he gave me...fuck, if that wasn't the best punishment I'd ever received.

His finger circled my entrance, pressed in.

Then he was pulling away and standing up, his hands going to his shirt, pulling it off, giving me a glimpse of that big, beautiful body. Squeezable pecs, the slightest covering of hair, shoulders I could grip, arms that were lean and lined with muscle as he shoved at the waistband of his sweats, and my gaze traced the thin trail of hair I knew led down to the hard cock that would be my salvation. His muscles rippled, rolling across his torso, up over his stomach, his—

"Your ribs!" I gasped, sitting up abruptly, desire gone in an instant, the chains rattling and parting and—

He prowled toward me, those sweats hanging low. "It's nothing."

"Honey, your whole side is black and blue! You need ice and bruise cream and—"

His hand went to the middle of my chest, and he pushed me back onto the mattress.

The air huffed out of me in a rush, and then he was on top of me, mouth hitting mine, tongue driving deep, fingers going down to circle my clit, to slide inside me, to drive me insane in a way that had the need that had been tempered by worry to well up again, to fill every inch of me, to—

"*Oh*," I groaned, head dropping back to the mattress, hips bucking.

His thumb had slid into my ass while his fingers worked me, making me feel both full and empty. I wanted his cock there, and I wanted it inside me, and I wanted—

To come.

Yeah, that would be good, would be great, would be—

He pulled out.

"I—"

A grin. A nip to my bottom lip. A flick to my clit.

And then his sweats were on the floor with his underwear and his cock was out and the hard head of it was brushing against me.

But not in.

And—God—I wanted it in.

A hand on my hip, the other beneath my armpit, sliding me up until I was fully on the bed, my head resting on the pillows, and then he was crawling over me again, not stopping and thrusting deep, but moving up my body, cock bobbing, until it was an inch from my mouth. "Suck it," he ordered.

One of my favorite things—having his dick in my mouth. Still...

"Are you sure you want to risk giving me another order?" I panted, which took all the sting out of my threat. "My teeth are—"

His fingers wove into my curls. "I like your teeth."

"I—"

He took advantage of my parted lips and pushed into my mouth, not far, but I liked sucking his cock. In fact, nothing made me crazier than having the hard length of him at the back of my throat, his groans in my ears, the salty tang of him on my tongue. So, I sucked him hard and deep and—

He pulled out. "No, Rosie baby. *I'm* going to do it."

And he did, fucking my mouth, a hand in my hair, the other behind him, teasing my breasts, making me gasp and choke and swallow him down, making my pussy ache, needy as fuck, my hands inching toward my clit, desperate for some relief.

But they were trapped between his body and mine and I couldn't reach, could only hold on to his thighs and be at his mercy.

Liquid between my thighs.

Need burning in my belly.

His cock hard in my mouth.

Fuck, I was going to come, like this, trapped between his body and the mattress, his cock in my mouth, his hand playing at my breasts, my thighs desperately rubbing together—

"Don't," he growled, pulling back, a *pop* in the air when he broke suction, and then he was moving down, one leg hitched up and over his shoulder.

I gasped.

Because he'd pushed inside.

Not gently, quick and rough and *in*, so deep it took my breath away, even as the walls of my pussy protested, squeezing him, convulsing, or maybe that was because the bite of pain was mingling with the pleasure and I was a heartbeat away from coming.

He dropped his forehead to mine. "*Fuck.*"

"Joel, please."

"I never dreamed"—he drew out—"that I could"—pushed in —"have something like this"—out again, pausing, waiting, his eyes on mine. "I love you, sweetheart."

My heart stuttered, and I lifted a hand, brushing lightly through his beard, something inside me settling, easing, but also tightening, growing stronger. And he seemed to feel it too, the threads connecting us increasing in number, in strength, time slowing and stretching, becoming just him and me, just this moment.

Just *us.*

Eyes stinging, I held his face, held on as he moved slow and steady, as he kept me in this cocoon of feeling, of love.

The outside world didn't matter.

The petitions and Phoebe and Willow and my dad and the truth that had begun settling in my heart—that maybe I didn't want my life to keep being my life, that maybe I wanted to take a beat and think about what *I* wanted.

That maybe I wanted to be different.

That different would be okay.

Because I had Joel.

"I love you," I whispered and watched his expression gentle, his eyes warm.

This man was mine.

Until the sun settled on our lives and we were ash and—

"Rosie."

I pressed my hand flat on his jaw, held him tight and he rocked against me, as we both took our time ascending toward the peak, toward the point that would have us both tipping into pleasurable oblivion.

But it was coming, slow and steady and inexorably.

Like the love that had wound through us, bound us together.

Forever and always.

THIRTY

JOEL

She was quiet.

She was hiding it well, but I knew her, knew this woman who had my heart, so even though she'd been up and gone when I'd woken up and had worked the rest of the day, I'd noticed.

And waited, through dinner, through planning time.

Waited for her to share with me.

She didn't, just pressed a kiss to my head as I watched some plays on my laptop that Coach wanted us studying, and went to bed.

I'd given her that play.

We'd been up late the night before—or really, very early that morning.

We'd shared something raw and open and *us* that had left my heart tender.

I could let her have some time.

Unfortunately, Billie was good at avoiding *and* keeping her distance (and compartmentalizing things that she thought weren't important if they would make it easier for me). Because she continued to do so all the way through the next day.

I needed to watch that, to make sure our relationship didn't seesaw back the other direction. Had to ensure I didn't become her project, her person to take care of.

She needed to accept I would take care of her in return.

That was the only way it could work for us.

That was why I'd decided to take matters in my own hands, even forgoing my pregame nap to drive over to the Civic Center, to park next to her car at City Hall and to climb the stairs, already preparing my ways to coax and encourage and maybe pleasure my way into that big, beautiful brain of hers.

Only, I didn't expect to find what I found at the top of the stairs.

Her assistant, Bella, was there, hard at work as always, her desk littered with papers and pens and pencils. She smiled up at me briefly then glanced back down at her papers. "Billie's in a meeting, but her office is open."

"Thanks, Bells," I said, rapping my fingers lightly on her desk as I went by.

Another smile, and then I was heading to Billie's office, my eyes drifting to the windows of the conference room as I walked, catching on blond curls and—

"What the fuck?"

Because it wasn't *just* blond curls. There was also a head of straight, blond hair on a lean body that I'd once known intimately—

Willow was standing next to my Rosie, both of them looking at a pile of papers on the table.

"What the fuck?" I whispered or maybe said aloud or—

I don't know.

Either way, both of their heads jerked up, and I found myself on the receiving end of two sets of eyes—but only one pair went wide, something like guilt flashing in their blue depths.

And it wasn't fucking *Willow.*

Hurt blasted through me, a bomb detonating without warning, and I turned on my heel, started back down the hall. Did Billie think I was so fucking incapable that I would make the same mistakes again? That I'd seriously continue to fuck up my future like I had five years ago? So much so that she'd felt the need to work her "magic" and get Willow to sign the papers?

"Joel!" Billie Rose's voice echoed down the hall, but I kept walking past Bella's desk, pounding down the stairs and out the front door. "Joel!" she called again, closer now.

"Forget it," I muttered, turning in the direction of my car. "Just go back to cleaning up my mess. I'll catch up with you later."

"I—" Her voice wavered, but then grew more determined as she matched my pace. "I don't know what you think you saw in there, but—"

"You mean you *weren't* with Willow in the conference room getting her to sign the divorce papers because I couldn't?"

That had her step faltering, her brows dragging together.

"What are you talking about? I wouldn't do that."

I shot her a look. "Rosie, come on. I saw you two through the window."

"It's not that." She blew out a breath. "That's not…" A wave of her hand. "What you think it was," she finished lamely.

I shot her a look. "So, what was it?"

She bit her lip, glanced away.

I waited…then waited some more.

"Right." I shook my head, started walking again, kept going until I made it to my car, yanking at the handle to unlock it, yanking again so it opened and I could climb in. "It's fine, Rosie," I said with a sigh, turning back to her. "Really," I added when she would have protested. "You've obviously got it covered, and if it gets us out of this shit, then it's all good with me."

"Joel, I—"

I paused again. *Waited* again.

"Let's just talk later," I said, turning away again, not wanting to see the stark expression on her face, not wanting to feel what I felt.

Which was betrayed. And hurt. And like she was throwing barriers up again.

After what we'd shared.

After the love and that long, beautiful moment in our bedroom, our hearts fully meshed...and she couldn't even talk to me?

Her hand gripped my forearm, rotating me back to face her, the fingers of her other hand coming to my beard, stroking lightly, giving me a brief, powerful surge of hope.

"Honey," she began—

Her cell rang.

"Don't," I whispered.

She swallowed and looked away, and that sinking feeling grew. I was in a moat, slowly drowning, slowly being sucked down into the mud.

Until I would be completely submerged.

Until I wouldn't be able to breathe.

Until I would cease to exist.

"It's not what you think," she whispered.

"Then tell me. *Talk* to me," I pleaded as her cell kept ringing. "Rosie baby, please just talk to me."

Her eyes came back to mine, and the sinking feeling grew.

Two steps forward, seventeen back, a few weeks of great and then this...feeling like I was on the wrong side of those sturdy barriers, excluded and barricaded and—

She dropped her hand and started digging into her pocket. "I'm sorry," she whispered, glancing at the screen. "I have to take this." And then she swiped at her phone and put it up to her ear.

"Hello? Yes, I'm still here." She turned away, put several feet between us. "Yeah. Yeah. Okay, I'll be right there."

Christ.

She hung up.

And I couldn't stay away, couldn't keep my distance, not with her, *never* with her.

No matter how much it hurt.

"Rosie," I said softly, settling my hand on her shoulder. "Just talk to me."

Her head tipped forward, chin dropping to her chest. "Joel," she whispered.

My fingers tightened. "Please, sweetheart."

A long moment then, "It's such a mess."

Relief coursing through me. "Just...start at the beginning, and we'll figure it out together."

She'd started to turn, but my words had her freezing, her shoulders slumping. "I'm not trying to go behind your back about Willow." A glance up at me. "I promise."

That had the hurt that had been pounding through me disappear, worry taking its place. I stepped closer, cupping her jaw. "What is it then? What's the matter?"

Her eyes came to mine. "Can we talk about it later? After the game?" she added quickly. "I'll tell you everything, I just..." Her phone started ringing again and she sighed. "There are fires everywhere that I need to put out."

I brushed the back of my knuckles over her cheek, worry swirling with guilt for adding to what she was dealing with, for being all sensitive and running off without taking a moment to consider this woman and all we were building. "After the game." I kissed her forehead, exhaled. "I'm sorry."

A shake of her head, those curls bouncing. "It's not you." She rose on tiptoe, pressed her lips to mine. "I promise. Work is just..." Another shake.

"Go," I whispered. "I'll see you tonight."

She nodded, dropped back down onto her heels, then went back inside.

I headed home and got a shit nap, played my game (and played it *off* my game because of that shit nap and the fact that Billie wasn't in the stands), then drove back to the house.

Only seeing the note after I'd pulled into the garage and dropped my shit on the kitchen counter.

Had to go to Sacramento for an emergency meeting with the governor. I'll be back as soon as I can so we can talk.
-Rosie

I pulled my phone out and called her.

Got voicemail.

I stayed up. Late into the night, well past the sun rising.

But she didn't come back.

Not that night.

Not that morning.

And I had no choice but to drive to the rink and get on the fucking bus.

THIRTY-ONE

BILLIE ROSE

Getting reamed by the governor wasn't on my list of fun free-time activities.

The only thing that made it better was the fact that the governor was a very busy woman and she believed me when I told her we'd done our best in the aftermath of the fire to follow all policies and procedures.

I thought she appreciated me not trying to bullshit her, not trying to pretend I was a perfect, infallible person, with a perfect and infallible team beneath me.

We were human and made mistakes and—

Well, anyway, thankfully, the governor only had fifteen minutes to both yell at me and listen.

It had been...not fun, very *not* fun.

But I'd gotten through it, and now I was just hitting the outskirts of River's Bend.

Joel's bus had already left, and I'd broken a promise.

To talk to him.

To trust him.

But it wasn't like I'd wanted to—shit was just hitting the fan and I had a job to do and...fuck, how many times in one lifetime did a woman get called in to a meeting with the governor?

That was—probably, hopefully—a onetime thing.

Definitely hopefully, considering the yelling.

I'd call him when I got back to the house, tell him everything.

Except, he was on the bus and that was a bad idea, to unpack all that shit with his teammates around. He'd be on edge and awkward and—

I'd go to the house, text him, promise to explain when he got back.

"Right," I whispered.

It'd be okay. I could make up for yesterday, for the hurt. It was just...complicated and chaos and Phoebe was making trouble and Willow had been in the conference room alone with my things.

I'd needed to talk to Joel, but I'd also needed to cover my ass—

Because I didn't trust Willow.

Now if I thought for one minute I could get her to sign those papers without it having an impact on the audit, I'd be all over it.

But I didn't.

So, I had to keep my distance from it, had to let Joel and Amy handle it.

Once I explained it to Joel, he would understand. He'd get it. He'd—

I drove through town, the streets quiet post morning school rush, winding my way to Joel's house—to the home that had become ours. Dating someone. Loving someone. Moving in with them. So much more complicated than just fucking them—

A horn blared behind me, and I blinked, frowning when I glanced up at one of the two signals on this end of town and seeing it was still red.

Yeah, I was tired, but not tired enough to be driving unsafely.

I'd functioned on *way* less sleep than this and—

The horn went again.

"Jesus Christ," I muttered, looking into my rear view before flicking my eyes forward again, seeing the light was still red. And considering I was taking up one lane of the two-way road, my only option was to pull onto the street on my right.

Either someone was in a really big hurry or—

The horn blared a third time.

Or they wanted to talk to me.

I signaled, turned right, cramming my little SUV onto the shoulder as much as possible, then waited, watching as the car followed me, my car still in drive, my foot on the brake, but prepared to hit the gas.

Because while River's Bend was safe, I'd seen too many murder documentaries.

Which was why I continued to watch as the driver's side door on the car behind me swung open, as...

My father stepped out.

And I knew that my day, my night, my fucking *morning* was about to get longer.

———

"Here you go," I muttered—yes, *muttered*—because I was tired and I'd had to fight, literally *fight* to get him back into his car and to follow me to Joel's place so I didn't have to have whatever "conversation" he needed (yup *needed*) to have with me on the edge of the road.

I preferred my berating with a side of caffeine.

"Nice place." He picked up the mug, took a sip, and made a face.

So apparently, I couldn't even make coffee right.

"It's Joel's place," I said. "He'd built the home right before the fire—and well, we're in the rebuild now. But yes, it is nice."

My dad grunted, took another sip of the coffee.

Couldn't be all that bad then.

I chugged my own cup of coffee, which I'd loaded with creamer (hazelnut was my new addiction, yum), and then refilled my mug, doctoring it up like before, but sipping it more slowly because the first punch of caffeine had hit my bloodstream.

What I didn't do was talk.

Because my dad had a reason for approaching me. I just wasn't going to play his game by asking him why.

For one, I didn't have the energy to do so.

For another, I didn't have enough fucks to give.

"You're not him, BR."

My nostrils flared. So, we were getting right down to it then, huh?

"You keep trying and trying and you'll never be him."

Yup. Definitely getting down to it. *Right* there in the jugular.

"That's the thing, *Dad*," I said, even though he'd been nothing like a fucking father. Not ever. Distance and appearances and pretending he didn't hate me.

But that was the thing about kids—we knew. We picked up on the disdain, on the undercurrents, and we tried to tiptoe around them, to swim through them without making a splash or drawing notice, but we were aware of every minuscule change in the flow of water, and every *single* action was calculated because of what we were picking up on.

To not think through every single angle would bring—

"I'm not my brother. I'm not Billy. I won't ever be." I sighed, picked up my mug again. "You just weren't paying attention." A sip. "I stopped trying to be him a long time ago."

He stilled, the mug close to his lips. "Bullshit."

"But," I went on. "I didn't actually give up on you until my office a couple of weeks ago. You see"—I set my cup down—"I actually had *hope*, after Joel stood up for me at dinner, after I realized I could stand up for me too, that I didn't have to take your shit because of something that wasn't my fault." I laughed, and it was bitter. "But I thought maybe I wouldn't have to. I thought you'd seen, that you understood how much I put into being a woman you could be proud of."

He scoffed, sipped again.

"Yeah," I said coldly. "I see that was stupid now. I got back into the pattern of believing that façade you and Mom were putting on meant you were trying to turn over a new leaf, that things would be different."

He scowled. "Some things don't change."

I froze, finger looped through the handle of my mug. "You know, that might be the most honest thing you've ever said to me."

His eyes narrowed.

I finished my second cup of coffee, knowing there was no way I was going to sleep now—not with the caffeine hitting my system, not with this pleasant little convo bouncing around my mind. "Now," I said, plunking the mug into the sink, "why don't you hit me with the lecture so we can both get on with the rest of our days?"

Those eyes narrowed further, but he opened his mouth, as though he was going to comply.

And seriously? He was delusional.

But sure enough, he commenced lecturing. "That bearded bastard is bad for you."

My brows lifted, any amusement I'd begun feeling disappearing. "Jesus, really?"

"He's still fucking married, for fuck's sake! What kind of slut lives with a married man?" He grabbed his mug, coffee sloshing up near the rim. "Not a daughter of mine. Not a smart, intelligent woman. Not a—"

I snatched the cup from him, turning on my heel, taking it to the sink and setting it inside.

"You're right," I said, suddenly not hurt or angry or dismayed. I was just...resigned. This relationship would never be what I wanted or need and it would never be what good for me. "I'm not a daughter of yours. Not any longer."

His mouth opened. Closed.

But he didn't reply, not then, not as I strode to the front door and pulled it wide, telling him, "You can go now."

Not when, after a long, drawn-out moment, he got up from the stool and walked out of the house.

Out of my life.

And my rage was so all-encompassing that I didn't put the pieces together.

Not right then.

Not until later.

But I *should* have known.

Thirty-Two

JOEL

The bus trundled into the rink's parking lot, bouncing slightly as it navigated the turn and pulled up to the curb.

I glanced at my cell, at the text from Billie, the one she'd sent ten minutes before.

I'm still up and ready to talk.

Finally.

Finally getting to the bottom of this shit. Finally getting her to stop throwing up barriers and talk to me and—

I was going to be calm and listen and not flip out, not be hurt.

There and open, not worried that the past was repeating itself.

And it wasn't.

Because she was home and waiting for me and willing to talk.

Except, last time she'd promised to talk, she hadn't been there when I got back to the house.

"Except, asshole, she had a meeting with the fucking governor," I said under my breath. I knew my Rosie couldn't exactly delay the governor to talk to her boyfriend or control when a summons came.

It still sucked.

But thankfully, I kept my muttering about it quiet enough that Fox didn't hear.

Or worse, Ry.

Who'd been studying me like I was a bug under a microscope for the last few days—becoming hyper focused when I'd played like shit a couple nights before. Thankfully, I'd had my shit together at tonight's game—or the previous night, anyway, considering it was well past midnight.

Sometimes we stopped at a hotel if the drive was too long.

But for the most part, we all—coaches, players, training staff, equipment guys—just wanted to get home and sleep in our own beds, see our partners, eat our own food, shower in our own bathrooms. Travel was all well and good until it was for half a year and not for vacation and—

The bus drew to a stop, the brakes whooshing as our driver, Kenny, put it into park. A second later, the door opened with a creak and the lights flicked on, and we all started coming to life, putting away earbuds and headphones, gathering up our shit, stuffing it into bags, standing and stretching with moderate groans.

Because it was the middle of the night.

Because we were all stiff and our asses were numb and legs were sore.

But we were home.

Thank fuck for that.

I took my turn shuffling down the walkway, stepping down the stairs, getting the fuck off the bus. The night air was cool and still, not even the barest hint of wind ruffling through the leaves of the trees that had been placed in the concrete diamond planters dotting the parking lot.

It felt like a beginning, as though I was on the cusp of something—

And hopefully that *something* was Rosie and me getting through this hurdle of whatever she was keeping from me.

A positive omen.

A—

"Hey." Ry's voice was quiet as he stepped off behind me.

"What's up?"

His brows lifted. "What's up with you?" he asked, drawing close as I started to walk toward my car.

I glanced over at him. "We're doing this now?"

"We're not doing anything," he said, keeping pace. "I'm asking what's up and, for once, you're not throwing up walls to keep me at a distance."

I froze.

What the fuck?

I was doing that?

Throwing up walls and creating distance and generally doing the shit that my Rosie was—the shit that fucking *stung?* That hurt like hell because I just wanted to know every part of her?

But...did she know every part of me?

Had I given her that chance?

"Shit," I muttered.

"What?" Ry asked.

"Nothing." A sigh when my teammate opened his mouth, probably to push me on my lie. "Okay, fucking *something*," I muttered. "I'm having a goddamned epiphany over here."

"Um..."

"And no, I don't want to talk about it, okay? Not at three in the morning," I added, when his brows furrowed. "I'll tell you later about how you got my head on straight, yeah?"

"Is this about the deserving more pep talk from the other day?" Ry punched his shoulder. "Because I'm not sure I meant it."

"Fuck you." I punched him back. "And it's not that, or not

only that," I muttered. "It's the shit about distance and walls and
—I didn't realize I did that, yeah?"

His brows came up. "*You* didn't realize you did *that?*"

"Like I said," I gritted. "Fucking epiphanies, yeah? And also,
it's really easy to be the one who's doing the taking care of
everyone else. It's hard as fuck to be the one who's sharing all the
shit that's twisting them up inside."

"But you shared it with me." A beat. "Kind of, anyway."

My stomach began churning. Because I had. Kind of. With
him and Fox on that fucking bus. But had I really broken it down
for my Rosie?

I wasn't sure.

And yet, she'd cried in my arms, shared about her brother, her
parents...and I hadn't even told her I'd been married before, hadn't
shared all the times I'd gotten my heart broken.

Hadn't—

I shoved a hand through my hair. "I need to go. I need to talk
to her."

"Yeah," Ry said. "I think you do." He nodded and stepped
back, let me beeline to my car. I bleeped the locks, tugged open my
door, was just sitting down when he called, "When in doubt, be
open!"

I waved, heart thudding, and sat down, knowing up until two
minutes ago I would have been certain *I'd* been the one who was
an open book, the one who always needed to shove through each
and every barrier to get to the heart of her because I was so fucking
open.

And now...I knew that was bullshit.

We all had barriers up, walls to get through.

Including me.

Something else to work on.

Add it to my poor me pity party for one and the bunch of
fucking baggage I was lugging around. I was a catch. *The* catch.

"Go me," I muttered, sighing as I put my car into drive, as I wove my way through the parking lot and turned out onto the main road that led through town, both bracing myself and heart for the conversation ahead.

Not running.

Finally.

Neither of us.

And my epiphany meant I could approach our conversation from a different angle, from knowing that I needed to do something different.

That I didn't just need to *be* something different, but that I *wanted* to.

"You got this, man," I murmured, turning off Main Street and heading for the edge of town, for my house, for my future.

Pausing at a stop sign before hitting the winding road to the housing development.

Checking for traffic. Right. Left. Right. Pulling forward—

Which was the moment I saw it.

There on a slightly sloping hill, perched like a placard declaring what the next festival was.

Only it wasn't promoting *Earth Day* or *May the Fourth Be With You*—

She was open. Ready to talk.

Fucking *really?*

And that was the point my vision hazed over.

I hit the brakes, screeched over to the side of the road, and...I was out of my car before I'd even processed moving.

———

The door slammed behind me, loud enough to shake the entire house like a fucking six-point-nine earthquake had hit, but I barely noticed that or my Rosie running down the hall in a pair of short cloth shorts and a tank top with no fucking bra, concern etched in her face.

A fact that didn't temper my rage at all.

I stormed toward her, barely noticing when she flinched back.

Because I was focused on what I was carrying, on what I'd ripped up from the side of the road.

"Joel?" she whispered, eyes wide, voice barely audible.

My temper spiked and my eyes were narrowed, my voice as loud as that door slam. "What the fuck is this?"

And then I threw the sign at her feet.

The blue and yellow letters spelling out:

Recall Billie Rose.

THIRTY-THREE

BILLIE ROSE

I stared at the piece of flimsy cardboard that had fluttered down to land on my feet.

And I couldn't really process what I was reading.

Then I did...and my first thought was, *What the fuck?*

Because seriously, *what the fuck?*

"What is that?" I whispered.

"What is that?" he thundered. "What is *that?*" He stepped forward, his big body towering over mine, his eyes flashing a deep emerald green. "Why don't you tell me what the fuck *that* is? It'll hold, honey," he drawled in what was a shockingly close impersonation of my voice. "We'll have time to talk about it later." He jabbed a finger at the sign. "*That* is not something to talk about later. *That* is something you talk about immediately, whether I'm on the fucking road or at home or on the goddamned moon."

I—

The sharp words shouldn't fill my belly with butterflies.

He was yelling and, in my face, and—

"Honey," I began, reaching for his jaw, his beard, intending to brush my fingers through it like I always did.

He liked it.

I knew he did.

Because his body always stilled and he rocked forward slightly on his toes, his eyes sliding closed as though my touch was nirvana. But right then, before my hand could make contact, before my fingers could brush through the coarse strands, he stepped back.

That distance...*ouch*.

"Don't *honey* me," he snapped, jabbing a finger at the sign again. "Just tell me what the fuck is going on with that?"

And...I'd had enough.

I lifted a brow, waited, and when he seemed like he was going to control himself, I said, "I don't know what's going on with that. The sign"—I did some finger jabbing of my own—"that's the first I've seen of it, and clearly that's a big fucking problem." I sighed. "But that's not one of the problems I've been waiting up to talk to you about. And"—I blew out a breath—"I don't appreciate the tone and the getting in my face and the throwing stuff at me."

His expression changed, and he stepped closer.

Only this time, I was the one who retreated.

I lifted my chin. "I told you I was going to do better, told you I wasn't trying to hide anything from you." A breath. "And at first, the stuff I held back truly wasn't important—truly, it was just little shit, annoying shit. And then it got bigger, but your family was here and you were on the road and there wasn't anything I could do about it, so it *could* hold."

"Rosie baby—"

"I *wanted* to vent. I swear I did. But literally, there was nothing I could do to change it and our schedules weren't lining up and then when they finally were going to, you saw Willow at City Hall and assumed some stuff, stuff we were going to sort out after the game. Except"—I sucked in a breath, held it, trying to slow my words, my boiling anger—"I got called into a meeting with the fucking *governor!* Something I told you about because even though you were out of town, we still texted, and I let you know what was up as soon as possible."

"Sweetheart—"

"So *I'm* doing my part." I slammed a fist to my chest. "*I'm* stepping up and trying to put everything I have into us because I fucking love you and what we're building, and *you're* the one who's not doing the same—"

"You're right."

"And furthermore, I've been here and doing my best, and my dad showed up this morning, and I think that things are really over between us because he was just awful."

"Oh, Rosie baby, I'm sorry."

"*And* my meeting with the governor wasn't fun—like I told you—but it was really *not* fun because I got yelled at because of the audit, something I haven't even gotten to tell you about because *I* only found out about it before your parents came and it's extra bad because it's supposed to be run by an independent organization—which it is—*except*—" I inhaled again, releasing the air on a sharp exhale. "*Except,* the company running the audit is owned by my former high school bully. And guess what!"

"Sweetheart."

I didn't acknowledge that, nor did I acknowledge the fact that he'd come closer, that his palm was on my cheek now, his fingers just dipping into the mess that was my hair.

"*Guess. What!*" I snapped, poking his chest.

His expression was gentle, but I was still pissed.

Raging in here, throwing shit at me.

"What?" he asked softly.

"Her assistant is *Willow.*"

Now his face wasn't gentle, not in the fucking least. "What?"

"Yup. Willow is assisting Phoebe Connors, royal bitch and high school prom queen, who lived to make my life miserable." I smiled, but it felt brittle and fake...probably because it was.

"Willow—your supposed to be ex-wife who's not—has been at City Hall every fucking day with a million questions for me and the finance committee and the controller, asking Bella to pull files, and I've made so many damned spreadsheets that for once in my life I'm sick of them." I swung out a hand. "And *that's* a crime against humanity because I love spreadsheets and the organization they bring and—"

His finger pressed to my lips.

"Rosie baby," he murmured. "Breathe, sweetheart."

"That's hard to do with your finger over my lips," I muttered, the words slightly muffled.

"Yeah, I imagine it would be."

Ugh.

I wanted to be annoyed.

But his half smile was adorable, as was him asking tentatively, "Can I hug you? Since I kind of fucked up on the order of things when I came in?"

Double *ugh*.

"Yeah," I muttered, because he was adorable and because I really wanted a hug and because of Phoebe and Willow and the audit and the petitions and the goddamned meeting with the governor. And also the sign he kicked aside as he shifted, wrapping his arms around me.

What the fuck was that sign?

He tugged me closer and I melted, leaning against him, soaking in the warmth and the comfort and this man I *loved*. He softened too; the tension leaving his body, even as his arms drew me nearer, as he buried his face in my hair, inhaling deeply.

"I'm sorry," he said softly. "I've lost my mind—or I feel like I've lost my mind and I'm not doing anything right and you've been...fuck, sweetheart"—he pulled back, cupped my face in both my hands—"you promised me you'd be here, that you wouldn't run or keep your distance from me, and *I've* been the ones throwing up walls and not being open and—"

His eyes were damp.

And—shit—now mine were too.

"I'm afraid," he said. "I love you and you're here and you say you want me and love me too and you're *here* and"—a breath—"I keep waiting for you to leave me, keep expecting it, and that's on me, not on you, even though I've been making it *your* issue and—"

"Honey," I whispered. "It *is* my issue. I love you. We're an *us*, so of course it's my issue."

"I'm fucking us over and yelling at you and being a total dick who's so wrapped up in my own head that—" He tilted my head up, held my eyes. "I'm sorry."

My heart squeezed. "I'm sorry too."

Brows furrowing. "Why the fuck are *you* apologizing?"

"Because I should have just told you about everything instead of trying to keep things easy and peaceful, and it added to your worry."

"Worry you didn't know about because I didn't share?" he asked softly.

There was that.

"Exactly," he said, bending down to brush his lips over my nose.

"You're sharing now," I pointed out.

"Yeah." He straightened, tugged a strand of my hair. "Get ready to be annoyed with your sappy, over-sharing boyfriend."

My mouth tipped up. "I thought you were something *more* than a boyfriend."

He went still, but his eyes blazed, the palm still on my jaw flexing. "I am. I fucking *am*. Which is why I'm going to take you to bed, hold you close, and you're going to tell me everything about the audit and the petitions and the meeting with the governor and Willow and that bitch I already hate."

"Phoebe Connors," I supplied.

"Don't say her name," he said with a smirk. "She's the Bitch Who Shall Not Be Named."

The last of the knot in my stomach relaxed.

He was here. He was listening. He was scooping me up into his arms and holding me tight and carrying me to the bedroom.

I wasn't alone.

I wasn't the only one trying.

It would be okay.

Only, as he carried me from the room my eyes caught on the sign he'd brought home.

Recall Billie Rose.

And I thought that I might not be alone, but my name was the only one on the sign.

THIRTY-FOUR

JOEL

I opened the door, thinking that it was Billie and her hands were full, or hoping—really hoping—that it was a Girl Scout who'd shown up, trying to sell me cookies.

I wasn't really paying attention to the fact that it was the middle of the day, and all the Girl Scouts would be in school.

I was just drooling over the potential for Thin Mints.

So, Willow standing on my fucking porch was a surprise.

And not one I wanted.

"What the fuck?" I asked, yanking my earbud out and glaring at her.

She was working with the Bitch Who Should Not Be Named on the audit. There was no way she'd just randomly turned up in River's Bend after five years.

It was all connected.

I just couldn't figure out *how*.

A divorce. Dissension amongst the residents. Her dad. Phoebe. The petitions.

None of it seemed to be connected.

But my gut was telling me it all was.

My Rosie gave her heart and soul to this town, but she wasn't one to break the rules. When she'd told me about the audit last night, I'd known that she hadn't deliberately done anything outside the bounds of propriety. I'd been here in the aftermath of the fire, in the chaos and ruin, and I'd seen her live and breathe and *bleed* for the people of this town.

And she'd continued to do so during the rebuild.

And even now.

So, the audit was fucking insult, without the addition of Willow and Phoebe.

But being run by the woman who'd made *my* woman's school years a fucking nightmare, who'd done the shit Rosie had told me about to her and her friends—

Well, fuck her.

And then add in Willow.

Christ.

"I—" Willow bit her lip, hesitated, and seriously, I did not have time for this.

"What?" I snapped, fingers tightening on the doorframe. "Why are you here?"

Those teeth stayed pressed into bright pink.

I sighed, decided that I may as well try. "Are you here to sign the divorce papers?"

Wide eyes, a stumbling step back. "Di-divorce papers?"

Why was that a surprising question? "Jesus, Willow, what did you think I wanted to talk to you about when I asked you to meet a couple of weeks ago?"

"But"—another step back, hands going to the railing, gripping the top—"I told you I'd take care of that."

I ground my teeth together. "And what? Is it going to take another five years? We're done, Willow. We've been done—*you* wanted to be done."

"I—you don't understand."

I tossed my hands up. "Then tell me. Why? Why would you do that? Why wouldn't you sign?"

A shake of her head. "I-I told you I'd take care of it."

"The time to take care of it was *five years ago*. This shit has to end now. I have the papers, you'll sign them, and we'll both move the fuck on."

She stilled, eyes coming to mine.

"Okay?" I asked.

A steady, unblinking gaze.

"Willow!" I snapped and she jumped. "*Okay?*"

Her lips parted, pressed together. Opened. Closed again. Then finally, "Okay," she whispered.

Relief burning through me in such a rush that my legs shook, but I locked my knees, took a breath. "Good." I tilted my head toward the opening. "Follow me." I stepped back, allowed her to walk through the door, shutting it before moving around her and down the hall to Billie's office, where we'd left the papers when Willow had skipped out on meeting me.

She huddled in the doorway, her gaze drifting around. "This is hers?"

I glanced up from the filing cabinet, mostly empty because the vast majority of our paperwork before the last year was ash, trying to understand the context of the question given all of what Rosie had told me. I snagged a pen from the holder. "You can sign with this."

Willow jerked, and there those teeth went again. I couldn't believe that I'd once thought it was sexy, that I'd once bought the vulnerable, fragile act.

Right up until she'd dug in her heels to divorce me.

And I had the physical evidence of her not following through on that right in front of me.

Stifling a snort, I held up the pen, waggling it at her. "Willow. Read the papers. *Sign* the papers."

"This is her office?"

202 ELISE FABER

Christ. *That* was what she was asking?

"Yeah," I said. "Now sign."

A nod. Her feet moving as slow as a fucking snail as she inched her way over.

I strived for patience, for calm, for some sort of understanding to reconcile the woman I'd loved, who I'd been heartbroken to lose, with the one who'd shown up five years later with some sort of agenda while actively working against the woman I loved. But there were a shit-ton of tangled threads to this problem—especially when I'd answered the door really just wanting some Thin Mints —so I needed that patience, and I needed to follow this one strand through to the end.

To untangle it. Or cut it free.

Before I helped Billie free the rest.

Willow. The petitions and the audit. This Phoebe bitch. The recall sign.

It felt like the world was closing in, like Rosie and I were in that garbage chute with Luke and Princess Leia, the walls growing ever closer, ready to crush the woman I loved, crush me, leaving us both fodder for a garbage monster.

But Rosie...Christ, while I'd been in my head and worrying about getting hurt, she was—

Hurting. Anxious. Dealing with this shit.

So, *patience* as Willow all but crawled over. *Patience* as she slowly read one page after another, lips moving as her eyes ran over the words.

Patience knowing when she signed, this would be one thing off our plate, off *her* plate.

So, I kept quiet. The first page. Another. One by one by *one*. Until she reached the last sheet. The one that should have been the fucking quickest to process...

Because it was just a signature page, and my name was already scrawled on the line where I was supposed to sign.

Easy enough. Just pick up the pen and go.

"Willow."

Another jerk, as though she'd somehow forgotten I was there.

"Yeah?" she whispered.

"Here." I extended the pen again.

Her nostrils flared on an inhale, and her fingers shook, but she took the ballpoint, positioned it in her hand and put the tip to the paper, to the beginning of that line...

Where. She. Just. Needed. To. *Fucking*. Sign.

But the goddamned pen didn't move.

Not immediately and not after several long moments as my hold on my patience began to splinter and break—

The pen clattered to the desktop.

Her gaze turned up to mine, eyes wet, tears gathering on her lashes, spilling down her cheeks. "I-I-I *can't*."

"Willow—"

One second, she was leaning over the desk, the next her body was slamming into me, her mouth crushing against mine, hands on my head, yanking me to her and—

I shoved her back, wiped the back of my hand across my mouth. "Jesus, what the fuck?"

She was still crying, but now she turned away, hands in her hair. "I can't. I can't. I can't!"

"Fuck it," I snapped. "My lawyer will just file the contested divorce petition, and we'll get it done that way."

Willow spun slowly on her heel. "I— Joel— *Wait!*"

"No. Christ. I don't get this." I waved a hand between us. "I don't get what the fuck *that* was, but I don't want any part of it, yeah? And you can fight me on the divorce, can draw this shit out, punish me for something I don't fucking understand when you're the one who wanted it in the first place, but I'm done waiting to start my future. I love Billie and I'm going to be with her. *Not* you!"

"I—" A sharp shake of her head, tears dripping along her jaw. "You don't understand."

"No, I don't, but I don't give a fuck anymore and I'm out of patience. Either sign the fucking papers or get the fuck out."

Her breathing hitched. "Joel, I need you."

"No, Jesus fuck. I already told you. We're not going to be together. Not ever again." I snatched up the papers, thrust them at her. "Now just sign the fucking papers so we can move on!"

"I can't!"

"Why?" My voice was rising, and I barely resisted the urge to grab her, to shake some fucking sense into that brain of hers. "We're not getting another chance. Our marriage is over—"

"I don't want to be married to you!" she screamed.

I froze.

Blinked.

"Then why the fuck won't you sign?" I roared back.

THIRTY-FIVE

BILLIE ROSE

I just wanted a coffee.

I *so* did not want to see Phoebe Connors taking up space at the counter of *my* coffee shop, chatting with the baristas, pretty and flawless and responsible for getting my ass called in for a reaming in the governor's office.

But this was my town.

And I wanted a damn coffee.

So, I moved to stand in line, debating between getting a pastry that pretended to be healthy (because it had fruit on it) or skipping right beyond that and going for the chocolate croissant—

"Your usual, Billie?" Donna called.

I blinked, looked up from the case of pastries I was drooling over, and smiled, turning in the direction of my usual table. "Yes, thanks, and a chocolate croissant."

"Sure thing."

Phoebe had turned, and I braced, expecting a snide comment about my choices, about counting calories. We'd gone to school in the time of heroin chic. Skinny was everything—collarbones defined, thigh gap evident, and heaven forbid someone have rolls when they bent over.

I'd always been curvy.

Because I liked tacos.

And chocolate. And donuts. God, donuts were *so* good. And cake was my favorite food and even if I could have dieted my way into a body like Phoebe's—which would have required rib removal and limb lengthening—I wouldn't have had the willpower.

I loved food.

I'd come to terms with feeling like I wouldn't measure up to her long ago—probably because I'd had plenty of experience in that department. But even though I'd let that go, she'd never changed. She'd always been cold and snobby and—

"I know you don't like me."

I blinked, only this time it wasn't because of pastries, freezing with my hand an inch above the chair's back, intending to tug it out, to sit down and enjoy my coffee despite Phoebe's invasion. We were adults on opposite sides of a problem, but we were still adults.

We could coexist.

But Phoebe hadn't stayed at the counter chatting. She'd come over to me, to my table.

And was making statements.

I pulled out the chair, sat down. "I don't know what you're talking about, Ms. Connors."

Phoebe plunked her cup on the table, took the chair across from me. "You know exactly what I'm talking about, Ms. *Donovan.*"

"I—"

Donna brought my coffee then, along with my chocolate croissant, and it stopped me from snapping back, gave me a minute to pause, to think, to study the expression on Phoebe's face.

"Thanks," I said as Donna straightened.

She winked. "I'll bring you a refill in ten."

"You're a goddess."

Donna chuckled and whisked off to another table, picking up empties before heading back behind the counter and doing something at the espresso machine that looked and sounded complicated, but—I knew from personal experience—tasted delicious.

Yet none of that explained why Phoebe was sitting across from me.

"Why do you think I don't like you?" I asked quietly.

She huffed out laugh. "Is that a joke?"

"You're the one who doesn't like me." I ripped off a piece of my croissant, shoved it in my mouth. "You've hated me and made it a point to make my life miserable since kindergarten!"

She rocked back in her chair. "What are you talking about?"

"My tie dye lunch box with the purple zipper?"

She frowned. "What?"

"And my scented pencils. And the fact that you shoved me off the monkey bars, made me fall and break my arm! I spent the whole summer in a cast and couldn't go swimming or do any of the fun camps."

"Billy Foster pushed *me*," she snapped. "I bumped into you and fell off and sprained my ankle."

Oh.

I hadn't known that.

"*And* I missed my dance recital."

Okay. I hadn't known that either.

But, "My science fair project?" I asked. "I saw you put it in the trash."

She went straight to affronted. "It was leaking everywhere, and Mr. King told me to!"

Damn...that seemed likely. My volcano project had been messy and— "That doesn't explain the glitter glue in my curls," I pointed out.

"Okay"—she winced—"*that* was me being a bitch, but I did it because I heard you telling Bailey that *I* was a bitch, so I decided that I might as well as live up to the name and—"

Damn. Because that was also true. I'd bitched to Bailey about Phoebe a lot. A *lot*. "What kissing Matt Hensley?"

Her nose wrinkled. "He kissed *me,* and it was my first kiss and it was freaking gross! I didn't ask for it and it was awful and I didn't want to kiss anyone for months afterward."

I jerked my head back. "Really?"

She nodded. "He slobbered all over me and jammed his tongue in and—" She shuddered. "It was gross and unwelcome and—" Her throat worked. "I didn't want it."

Sympathy was *not* blooming in my stomach. It *wasn't*.

"What about prom?" I asked, determined to hold on to my grudge.

Regret on her face—and maybe it was fake, but my bullshit detector wasn't activated, hell, it hadn't blipped to life at *all* during this conversation. "Bitch again," she whispered.

Ugh.

Was I seriously feeling a bit sorry for this woman?

Because a lot of this was a series of misunderstandings?

Ugh.

I picked up my mug, processing this, drinking deeply, buying myself time, trying to process that the truth I'd held tight, that had warmed the fire in my belly to hate this woman, had fostered with grudge might not be so simple. And that...made me angry. Or sad. Or—

"I thought you hated me," I whispered.

She inhaled, seemed to be studying me as closely as I was studying her. "No," she whispered back.

"But—" I broke off, took another sip.

It was a question I couldn't ask, *shouldn't* ask.

"What?"

I shook my head. "I don't know." I set my cup down, rubbed my temple. "And it doesn't matter, does it? We, um—I thought you didn't like me. You thought the same. We didn't get along and maybe it was a series of stupid kid shit and misunderstandings and grudge-holding, but—"

I wanted to ask why she was here leading the audit if she *didn't* dislike me.

If she didn't have a grudge, if she didn't want to make my life miserable, then why in the fuck was she here now, her company picking over every decision I made, trying to find a mistake?

"We're adults." I shrugged. "This stuff shouldn't matter. I didn't like you. You didn't like me. It was all a knotted mess of misunderstandings."

"But it does matter," she said softly. "To me too."

I found my lips turning up. "I want to say I'm all mature and I'm over it—and I am, I guess, but—"

"We're not unfeeling humans." A tilt of her head. "That stuff still stings."

More ugh. Because it *did*.

"For the record, I'm sorry for my part of it," she told me. "And I'm just here to do my job as quickly as possible so I can go back to my boyfriend." A sigh. "*If* I still have a boyfriend. We were supposed to go on vacation, and I had to cancel it to come up here and get this done and..."

"And he wasn't happy?" I asked when she trailed off.

"No." A rueful smile. "Probably because I've canceled this trip three times before for the same reason."

"Damn, that's cold," I whispered without thinking. Then winced again. "Shit. I didn't mean it like that," I hurried to say when her eyes clouded and pain danced across her face. "Whatever happened between us and the history I *thought* I knew—the history I'm currently sifting through in my head trying to under-stand—I know what it's like to work hard and enjoy your job and that's okay."

"I've seen the hours you pull," Phoebe said quietly. "I know you know what it's like to work hard."

—7

——

————

——

——

——

————

——

——

——

I hesitated, indecision in my belly, because this—all of this was a mind fuck of epic proportions—but then because I was me, I pushed that hesitation aside and reached over, squeezing her hand. "What I'm saying is that you don't have any apologies to make for working hard at your job."

A flare of pink on her cheeks. "Thanks."

"You're welcome."

And...silence between us, the normal noises of the coffee shop around us. Awkwardness descending. I shoved another piece of my croissant into my mouth, chewed, and swallowed. "Did...did we just have an actual nice conversation?" I asked to break the ice.

Phoebe chuckled. "I think we did."

She sipped. I sipped. That silence fell again.

Until I had to interrupt it. "I just have one question."

Phoebe tilted her head to the side, silken hair spreading like a golden sheet behind her. "Is it going to ruin our newly formed peace?"

"Is that what this is?" I countered.

Phoebe curled her fingers around her mug, her perfectly painted nails on display. "I was kind of hoping so." She smiled slightly. "I'd like to not have to avoid you when I come back and visit my parents."

I inhaled, took the olive branch she'd extended. "I'd like that too."

She nodded. "Okay."

"Okay."

"So," she said, "ask your question."

I straightened, nodded. "I was just curious why you had to cancel that vacation and come now."

She frowned.

"I mean, the papers weren't going anywhere. We didn't even know that a complaint had been filed and an audit ordered. You didn't have to come immediately."

Petitions. Audit. Recall.

It all was just too—

Pat.

Phoebe tapped her nails on the outside of her mug. "It's the same reason I had to hire Willow even though she doesn't have any experience. I might be the CEO"—she made air quotes—"but I'm far from the person calling the shots. The board is in charge, and when they say jump, it's been made clear to me that the only acceptable reply I can give is how high?"

THIRTY-SIX

JOEL

Willow opened her mouth—
A door slammed.
And her *mouth* slammed shut as she turned and started to run from the office.

I was faster, though, snagging her arm just as Billie's voice echoed down the hall. "Joel? You still home, honey? You would not believe—"

She appeared in the open doorway, eyes going wide. "Okay, well, apparently we both have things to share that aren't believable."

"Yup," I said dryly as Willow tried to jerk her arm from my grasp. "Apparently we do."

Her eyes went down, presumably to where I was holding Willow's arm, then came back up to mine. "Maybe you should clue me in first?"

"Probably." I guided Willow over to the chair, pushed her down into it. "Since she was going to tell me why she won't sign the divorce papers."

My Rosie inhaled then nodded, crossing to us, hesitating and then taking the second chair when I inclined my head toward it. I remained standing, still not convinced that Willow wasn't going to jump up and take off again.

Patience.

It existed solely in the barest wisps of emotion inside me. The slightest puff of air, and that tolerance would cease to exist.

"Willow," I prompted.

Maybe too harshly, but it seemed to snap her out of the fog, and she glanced toward me, toward Billie, saying, "I'm not trying to steal him from you. I promise."

Rosie's eyes cut to mine. "Okay," she said softly, "but to be fair, that's not the vibe you've been giving off with you calling yourself Joel's wife and refusing to sign the divorce papers."

"I can't divorce him." Willow dropped her head into her hands. "I can't."

"Why not?" Rosie asked.

"They said they'd help me if I didn't." A groan, fingers gripping the blond strands. "But they can't help me. Not really. Because it's all taking longer with COVID—"

I frowned.

"And I just need another six months, and it should all be g-good." Willow lifted her head. "I just need six months, Joel. If we get divorced now, the lawyer says I'll have to start over and—" She pushed out of the chair and I rocked forward, intending to stop her if she made a break for it. But she didn't, just stopped in front of me, eyes panicked. "I can't start over. It's been too long, and he needs me. I promise I'll sign whatever you need once I get the visa. I promise"—she dropped to her knees, wound her arm around my knees—"I *promise!*" She turned to Rosie. "I won't stand in the way of you guys. I just need the visa and I'll—I'll—s-sign. I swear to you, I'll sign!"

I tugged her off my legs. Not roughly, but I wasn't striving for patience any longer. I was confused as fuck, because...no, this wasn't an act. This was real and—

"Here," Rosie said, bringing a blanket over as I coaxed Willow back into the chair, wrapping the material around her legs. She dragged the other chair over, made eyes at me until I sat in it, my legs tangling with Willow's. Then she gently cupped Willow's jaw. "I need you to start at the beginning, honey."

Silence. Then, "I had a baby."

Shock ricocheted through me, patience on that razor-thin edge again. If I had a kid and she'd kept it from me—

"His parents didn't approve," she whispered, yanking me out of that thought. "They didn't want us to be together and me being pregnant didn't make them happy, so Anthony and I went to live with my mom—"

A mom she'd told me was dead.

Christ.

"And I had the baby, but Tony, h-he"—her voice broke—"he g-got in a car accident a few months later. I tried to make money for all of us after he died. I really tried, but it just...there was never enough, and when I got the offer to be an au pair, it was more money than my mom and I had ever seen. But I couldn't tell them that I had Andrei, not if I wanted the job."

She dropped her head into her hands again.

"It's okay," Rosie said softly. "Breathe. We're here. Take your time."

Willow lifted up, eyes red and swollen, makeup streaked all over her face. "It's not okay! My mom's sick, and COVID shut everything down, and all the government organizations are still backed up, and I *still* haven't gotten the visas yet!" Her lungs hitched. "And they should have come through by now, but I thought that before, thought I'd get them and could sign the papers and you wouldn't be any wiser, but I-I—" She scrubbed a hand over her face, smearing the makeup further. "They didn't, and if I don't get the visa now, it'll be too late. I need them to be able to come. My mom. Andrei—"

She dropped her head again.

"I just want to be with my baby."

Fuck. *Fuck.*

I looked up at my Rosie, saw the same conflict on her face that was surely on mine.

Though my Rosie was able to put hers aside and ask the appropriate question. "If the visas are in progress, why are you so worried about the divorce? You've been here long enough to get your green card."

Willow swiped at her eyes. "What?"

"Do you have your green card?"

Willow nodded. "Yeah."

"So, you didn't need Joel," Rosie pointed out. "You could have gotten them here on your own."

Teeth in her bottom lip, that fragility creeping back into Willow's demeanor. "The lawyer said it's faster to get them over here if I'm still married. And now, if we get divorced, because they haven't been approved yet, it will delay things, maybe start the whole process over. And I can't risk that." She reached for me. "Please, Joel," she begged. "I'm only asking for a little more time."

I glanced up at Billie, knew what her answer would be, even before our stares connected, and when they did, my heart expanded. For her. For this woman I loved.

Because hers was so big.

Because hers had been wounded and was vulnerable beneath the powerful barricades she'd erected, but she'd made space for me inside it, had made space for so many others within it, and now she was willing to make space for Willow and her baby and a woman she'd never met.

And even with all of that, she didn't lose her head.

Or her focus.

She made it clear she would be here for me, would support a

decision that would inconvenience her, for a person who'd lied and scammed and hurt her—

And me.

That truth struck hard, ringing through my mind.

Maybe I should say *fuck you* to Willow, should hate her, but…I couldn't, and I didn't. I was pissed, yeah, and wished she'd handled anything about this situation differently.

But I wasn't the kind of person who could fuck over someone innocent, someone sick.

Even if I *was* disgusted by what Willow did.

I'd need proof first, though. I was done with letting things ride and not checking up on them. Proof…and then I could give her that time.

I rubbed at my forehead. "Why didn't you tell me about them when we got married?"

She bit her lip. "I'd already lied. I said I was an orphan, and you didn't know about Andrei. I—" She swallowed. "How could you look at me as a wife when I'd left my son behind? My family?"

"I would have understood. Would have helped."

Maybe. Probably.

Hopefully.

"I don't know, Joel," she whispered. "I was grieving and messed up and living a damned lie. And I loved you and that hurt. I wanted a future with you and *that* hurt. Because I was supposed to be with Tony, and if I had feelings for you…that meant I was betraying him and what we had and—" She shoved her hand through her hair. "I *shouldn't* have had them. Shouldn't have loved you. So, I didn't let myself. I put distance between us and I—*God* —I was picking fights with you all the time and—" Her lips pressed flat.

"Eventually, you asked for a divorce," I supplied.

"I had to," she whispered. "I couldn't stay with you. You're not Tony."

Jesus. *That* felt great.

I pushed that aside. "But the divorce was the beginning of your problems once COVID hit."

A long pause before she said quietly, "It was. I held on to my paperwork, intending to sign and finish the filing once the visas came through." A sigh. "Only the world shut down."

"And now we're here."

"Yeah," she whispered. "We're here and it's my fault and"—she reached for my hand—"I'm sorry. Really, I am."

"Why come back?" Rosie asked abruptly.

Willow stilled. "I'm sorry?"

"You could have just let the clock run out," Rosie said. "Joel wouldn't have known. You could have continued on with your end of the paperwork and gotten the visas processed." Her curls bounced slightly as she tilted her head to the side.

"So why didn't you?"

THIRTY-SEVEN

BILLIE ROSE

Willow's eyes went wide. "He told me to."

"He?" I asked, mostly because while I felt sympathy for Willow and all she'd been through, could even understand why she taken it so far, her naming half the populace as the reason she'd come back to River's Bend and started all this shit wasn't exactly endearing. "He who?" I pressed when she looked back down at her hands.

"I don't know," she whispered.

"Not good enough," I said, keeping my tone neutral even as my frustration grew. "What is his name?"

Willow clutched her hands together. "I *don't* know."

Seriously?

"Okay"—a steadying breath—"so how do you know him?"

"I don't," Willow protested. "My attorney knows him, and she told me he has connections to get the visas processed faster. I just needed to do some work for him first."

"What work?" Joel asked quietly.

"He said his company was short of employees because of the

pandemic, and Phoebe needed help with a big project. He said if I came to River's Bend and helped her, then we would be even."

That made sense—and didn't because...

"But you were here before the audit."

Guilt on Willow's face, there and bright and *obvious*. "I needed to—" She shoved up to her feet. "Actually, I should go. I'll sign the papers," she said. "As soon as my family is here, I'll—"

"Yeah, no," I told her. "That's not going to work for me. *Why* were you here early?"

"I—" Her gaze darted away. "It doesn't matter. I didn't find anything—"

"Wait." Joel was on his feet now. "What do you mean, you didn't find anything?"

"I—" Panic had overtaken guilt. By a *long* fucking shot.

"Willow," Joel said, tone as cold as I'd ever heard it. "You can't expect me to help you with your problem if you're doing something to fuck over the woman I love."

She froze. "But—"

"*Tell* us."

"I—" She seemed to shrink in on herself.

Meanwhile, I was frantically trying to figure out how to get the information I needed to get without throttling her.

Willow could leave her kid behind and move to a new country, could struggle to get her son and mother here for five years, but she couldn't answer a question?

"Willow, *Willow.*" Joel snapped his fingers, catching her attention. "I swear to fuck, I will not lift a finger for you, no matter how sad your sob story is if you hold back now."

A shuddering breath.

Her shoulders caving in further, but she spoke. "I swear I don't know the man's name. He's tall and blond and American. Older. Maybe late fifties or early sixties. My lawyer just said he'd worked in the government for years."

Joel sighed.

Wide eyes. "That's all I know, I promise."

"Maybe," I said. "Except you haven't told us what you were trying to find in our apartment."

She was quiet, for too fucking long.

But then she looked down at her feet and said, "Evidence."

I frowned. "Evidence for what—" My sigh stoppered up the rest of my words. "Evidence for the audit, evidence that I'd done something wrong." A beat as she nodded, gaze still on her shoes. "Except, you didn't find any, did you?"

"No." A whisper.

"And the second time you showed up?" I asked. "More of the same?"

A shake of her head.

My pulse picked up. "No?"

"No," she murmured. "I was supposed to get you to leave again."

The possessive tone, the weird vibe, the *I don't want to be any trouble.* The way she'd stormed off when Joel and Fox and Dessie had shown up.

"So you could look?" I asked.

She shook her head, and my gut sank.

"So you could leave something behind."

Not a question because...it wasn't a question. I knew the answer the moment I'd begun to say the words.

Willow inclined her head.

"What?" I asked. "What were you supposed to leave behind?"

Willow bit her damn lip again.

————

"I just don't understand," I said, leaning back on the sofa arm and drinking deeply.

Joel sat next to me, my feet on his lap. "All of it's kind of

fucked, Rosie baby. So, what part in particular does my ridicu-
lously smart, exceptionally sexy woman not understand?"

How Willow didn't know what she was supposed to leave
behind in my apartment—other than it being an envelope.

How she didn't open it and look inside...because I sure as shit
would have.

How—more importantly—Willow could do what she had to
Joel.

And how Willow could leave her kid behind while doing it—
though, maybe I understood that more than the rest of it because I
knew that most mothers would do anything for their kids.

Except mine, of course.

Part of the reason I didn't want kids.

Because my mother's negligence, how she lived in a world that
only obliquely included me, wasn't the issue.

Willow leaving her family behind was.

So maybe I needed to amend my statement to not understanding how she didn't confide in Joel any of that.

Because the man was a fixer—he'd married her to keep her safe
legally, to keep her near him. The idea that he wouldn't have
accepted her son, her mother, was unfathomable. Willow could
have had it all.

He'd loved her.

And...she hadn't wanted him.

God, I knew what that felt like, how much it fucking sucked,
how it lingered and ate away and—

I put my wine down, touched his jaw, and focused on the more
important thing at the moment. "Are you sure you're okay?" I
asked. "After everything that happened today?"

I held my breath, half expecting him to shut me down.

But he was Joel. He'd learned from his mistakes.

"I'm not saying it feels great to learn all that shit," he muttered,
taking a pull of his beer and propping his feet on the table. "But
I'm glad we finally have some answers."

"Even if it has only led us to more questions?"

Joel sighed and leaned back against the cushions, one arm tucked behind his head. "Yeah. I think so, anyway. We know why Willow showed up here, and the timing makes sense, as does why she wanted the divorce. But—" Another sigh before he quietly went on. "Do I wish she felt like she could actually have an honest conversation with me about all of this at any point during the last five years?" He huffed out a breath. "Absolutely. But am I glad that I'm where I am at? Rosie baby, I can't imagine a better place on this planet than being at your side."

"Damn," I whispered.

"What?" he asked, turning his head on the cushion, eyes coming to mine, his expression soft.

"You've always made me feel too damned much."

Now his mouth curved. "I'm just thankful we've moved beyond hate."

Laughing, I shifted closer, resting my head on his shoulder.

"Now, Rosie baby," he murmured, running his hand through my hair. "What were you confused about before?"

I didn't make him work for it. "Why hire Willow for the audit?"

His fingers continued moving through my curls as he said, "That's the part that really doesn't make sense. She's always worked in childcare. She had the job as the au pair first, then was a preschool teacher after we got married." A rough chuckle. "She's used to potty training and finger painting, hates numbers and files and spreadsheets."

"The humanity," I muttered.

"I know that seems insane to you, my beautiful, organizational queen, but it's the truth." He sat up, keeping his arm around me as he reached for my wine and handed it to me.

"Yeah, I'm getting that."

"And she sure as shit wasn't equipped to be a spy."

"No," I agreed. "I don't think she is."

"So"—he leaned us both back again—"I don't understand why someone would want her to help the Bitch Who Shall Not Be Named with the audit, but I'm just glad we finally have some answers and can figure out how to move forward."

"Don't call her that."

His arm tightened, and he leaned up again, eyes flicking to mine. "Don't call who what?"

"Phoebe," I whispered. "I...I think I might have painted the past with too broad a stroke." I told him about the coffee shop and the conversation, what I'd learned and the misunderstandings and ownership and that she and I might be able to have a different future.

"Wow," he said when I'd finished. "So, we both really did have an eventful morning, huh?" He tugged at a curl. "Although I'm still inclined to hate her, just on principle."

I burrowed into him, giggling. "Thank you for that." A beat. "Really."

"You're welcome."

I snorted then kissed his jaw. "Seriously, though, I think...I think I want to give her a chance."

"I'm here, my Rosie baby. For whatever you need. Second chances or grudge-holding or anything in between."

I knew that.

I felt it.

I *believed* it.

THIRTY-EIGHT

JOEL

"Tell me how you conned me into yard work on my day off," my dad muttered.

"Rosie mentioned that she wanted to plant some flowers, but with everything going on"—I grunted when the tip of my shovel hit a rock—"she hasn't had time."

"That's what I like to hear my boy say." My dad paused in digging his own hole. "I just generally like to avoid the grunt work myself."

"Just saying"—I kept digging—"you usually love the grunt work."

"Just saying"—*he* kept digging—"you could afford to hire someone to do this for you."

I paused, looked up, lifting my brows at him. "Just saying *saying* that someone important to me taught me that things mean more when you put some effort in."

"Damn." He sighed. "I hate it when being right means I have to do more work." He began to work on another hole. "You can't pay someone to do this shit for you?"

"If I paid someone to do everything that was a pain in the ass, I wouldn't be able to afford this house," I pointed out.

A pause in the digging, his lips twitching. "Damn, I'm a good dad."

I snorted.

"No, seriously"—he moved on to another hole—"I do good dad." A grin up at me. "I mean, look how great my kids are. You. Kira and Avery and Delilah. All great. I'm a lucky motherfucker."

"Who gets to dig holes on an early weekday morning."

A shrug. "How else am I going to get my exercise?"

"Golf?"

"Meh. I'd rather be here with my son." A glance in my direction. "We don't see each other enough as it is."

Crap.

"Dad," I began.

He exhaled and clapped me on the shoulder. "That wasn't a guilt trip, Joey. I just...I'm glad we're here together. Now. And very aware, especially after the fire, of how precious this time is."

"Shit, Dad." My voice was bordering on rasp.

He squeezed my shoulder then went back to digging. "Too damned early for this shit, yeah?"

"Yeah." I put my shovel back to work. "But, Dad?"

A glance up at me. "Yeah?"

"Thanks for being willing to be here."

He went still then, "I love you, son."

My eyes burned a little, but it had to be the sun glaring down at me. Or emotions. Or baring my damned soul...and yup, it was way too early for this shit.

I was glad we were doing it, anyway.

"I love you, too, Dad—"

Gravel crunched, and I turned to see a car pulling into the driveway, a familiar pair in the front seats.

"Shit," I muttered.

"What?" my dad asked.

"It's Rosie's parents."

A glance in my direction. "That's a good thing. Your mother and I have been wanting to meet them."

"You say that *now*."

His brows lifted.

"But you haven't met them yet."

Now his brows furrowed. "They're that bad?"

"Her mom is...I don't know." I shook my head. "Off in her own world at the best, negligent at the worst. But her dad—"

I didn't get to that part of my explanation.

Because my Rosie's dad shoved his car door open and bellowed, "Hurry up! I want to get this shit done."

"Ah," my dad said.

"Yeah. He's..." I waved my free hand. "*That.*"

A pissed-off man marching over to us, not waiting for his wife, not helping her when she opened the trunk and pulled out a...

Huge basket that was almost overflowing.

Okay, that was weird.

Especially considering that Rosie had told me about the shit-show of her last interaction with her dad.

And her all but kicking him out of her life.

And now...he was walking across my freshly-laid sod and wasn't even carrying the basket that was weighing his wife down as she teetered toward us on heels that were equally as damaging to my freaking *lawn*.

"Right," my dad muttered, visually steeling himself. "How do you want to play this?"

"Spine, no fear, and"—I glanced at him—"if he says one bad thing about the woman I love then I'm going to dig a much bigger hole."

"I'll join you."

Billie's dad stopped in front of us with a huff then, but I didn't stop digging the hole I was working on—and I don't know if my dad was following my lead or throwing shade right beside me—but he didn't stop either, just kept plugging away on his.

"Uh-hum." An irritated throat clearing.

Slowly, I glanced up, met John's eyes, the blue the same color as my Rosie's, but the frosty depths not even fucking close to the warmth she radiated out to the world.

"John," I said, leaning on my shovel. "What are you doing here?"

"Where's my daughter?"

He was a bastard and had hurt my woman time and again, so, I didn't bother to sugarcoat my words. "I don't think you have a right to call her that."

A sharp inhale had me looking to the left, seeing that Billie's mom had come over. "Hi, Annie," I said gently, because as much as I disapproved of a lot of the way she'd handled things when it came to Rosie, I'd seen glimpses of something deeper when the fog around her demeanor cleared.

She swallowed hard. "Hi, Joel."

I inclined my head. "This is my dad, Rob."

My dad started to extend a hand, then stopped and shrugged. "I'll have to owe you a handshake when I'm not covered in dirt."

Annie's eyes drifted around. "Sunflowers?" A beat. "And hydrangeas?"

"Rosie wanted to add some color."

"Right." She shifted the basket to her other arm. "I bet it'll look beautiful."

"She's got a good eye," my dad supplied.

"And how would you know that?" Billie's dad snapped.

My dad slanted a look in my direction, brows flicking up, silently telling me precisely what he thought of John. "I've seen the inside of the house." A shrug. "That's all it takes."

Silence.

And somehow, I was desperate for this conversation to be over...so I could go back to digging holes.

Thankfully, my dad came to the rescue, leaning his shovel against the porch railing, and asking Annie, "Can I take that off your hands? It looks heavy."

"I—" Her gaze danced around then she nodded hurriedly. "Yes, thank you. It's just a housewarming gift for Joel's and Billie's new house."

"This is quite a haul," my dad said, stepping forward and gently taking it from her then walking it over to the porch and setting it down. "I'm sure Rosie and Joel will both enjoy it."

"We will," I agreed, eyeing the holes longingly.

"Y-you call her Rosie too?"

My dad froze, glanced at me.

I widened my eyes, having no clue why that had her expression turning distraught. "Look," I said quietly, "we've actually got a lot to do here."

John cleared his throat again, loud enough to make Annie jump. "Where's BR?" he boomed.

"*Billie Rose* is at work," I snapped.

"She works too much," Annie whispered.

"No. That girl is lazy," John retorted. "Never getting enough done. Always cutting corners and—"

"That doesn't sound like the Rosie I know," my dad said.

"She's a disappointment and—"

"*John! I'm not listening to you talk about our daughter like that again!*"

I blinked, shocked at Annie's tone.

"Excuse me," she whispered, pushing a curl out of face, the anger fading as quickly as it had come on. "I-I'm just...tired." Her gaze dropped to her feet then she seemed to have to brace herself before she glanced up again. "Please, just...pass the basket along. And tell Bill—*Rosie*—that I'm sorry I missed her."

"I will," I promised.

She hesitated, mouth opening like she was going to say something else, but then she seemed to sink further into that protective shell. "Bye, Joel. Nice to meet you, Rob." She turned on her heels, picked her way back to the car.

We weren't so easily rid of Rob. "You tell BR that I expect her to return my fucking phone calls before the week is out."

"I'll be sure to *not* pass that message along."

My dad chuckled.

John took a step toward me like he was going to do something really stupid.

Unfortunately—for me—he controlled himself, spun around, and stomped to the car, tearing out of the driveway and disappearing down the road.

"That man is a real dick," my dad muttered.

"Tell me about it." I stuck the edge of the shovel into the ground, leaned the handle against my chest, and used my arm to rub the sweat from my face.

"It's the mom you need to watch out for, though."

I blinked, glanced over at my dad. "What do you mean?"

"If she ever decides to come out of the fake world she's living in, she'll be dangerous as an adder." He walked to the porch. "So, you'd better make sure you're on the right side of the fangs."

"Jesus, Dad."

A shrug as he reached into the basket, rattled through a couple of tins, and pulled out a cookie. "It's decades of experience, son." He took a huge bite, chewed, swallowed. Then shrugged.

"She makes damned good snickerdoodles, though."

THIRTY-NINE

BILLIE ROSE

I'd gone in to work early, my mind racing too much with everything we'd learned.

Willow and Phoebe.

The board and the man who Willow didn't know.

The recall sign and the petitions and the audit and the divorce and—

The visas.

That was where I was starting—collaborating with Master Google and putting all my knowledge gained from watching a hundred and something episodes of *90 Day Fiancé* to work. Confirming the skeleton of knowledge I had and cross-referencing it with the articles I was reading.

Confirming what I knew in my heart.

Willow hadn't been lying.

About the visas or the divorce.

So that just left the audit and the man and the petitions and...

The recall.

Okay, so the recall was a matter of public record.

I could start there, could find out if it was really filed or just a random sign from some disgruntled resident. And if it *was* real, I should be able to find out who filed the paperwork, and then once I found out what I could about the recall maybe I could track down some information about Phoebe's company and the board and the mysterious man who wanted Willow to work with her and plant evidence and...

I rolled my head from side to side, shook out my hands.

Then I focused, and Google and I became intimately acquainted with every part of the recall process.

I dragged my finger across the screen, my heart sinking when I found—right there on the Secretary of State's website—proof that the recall was happening. I didn't know if they'd gotten enough signatures to actually force an election, but the papers had been filed and the process was in motion and it had all been done by...

"Roger Styles," I murmured, focusing on the name at the bottom of the page. "Who the fuck is Roger Styles?"

I knew everyone in my town, from human to dog and cat and miniature pig.

But I didn't know a Roger Styles.

I searched every social media platform, scoured every spreadsheet and database and volunteer form I had access to. I searched through my emails. Hell, I even located a phonebook and flipped through the S's (and the R's) looking for any indication of him.

Nothing.

Oh, I found men with the same name, especially on social media.

But, as far as I could tell, there wasn't a Roger Styles in River's Bend.

So, he wasn't a resident with a complaint—and further proof of that seemed likely because the address he'd used on the forms wasn't a real one.

A fake name. A fake address.

What was going on?

How had he been able to start the process without living here?

And further, when I began going through the petitions—not just looking at the pages and pages of signatures, but at the small description at the top of the first page—the organizer was listed as Roger Styles.

His name was on the papers protesting the school playground and also on the greenscape complaint and even the fucking objection to the soccer tournament.

Oh, and the library books too.

The first form that had been sent to the librarian wasn't from Karen and company.

It was from Roger Styles.

But who *the fuck* was he?

"Christ," I muttered, shoving away from my desk when a search of Phoebe's company came up empty. They had a website with a robust description of services and past clients, but there wasn't an employee directory or any mention of one Roger Styles.

And no social accounts in the area.

And...I wasn't sure what else I could pursue with my cyber sleuthing.

Google and I had become best friends, I'd now wasted hours of my day trying to find this man, and...I was no closer to any answers.

"Damn," I muttered, shoving in my keyboard and pushing up from my desk.

I needed coffee. Food.

Something I couldn't get with Joel because he was on the bus and headed out for his first playoff game.

One game down in Bakersfield.

One up here.

Then, depending on who won and lost, they'd play another game here in River's Bend.

The playoffs were different from the NHL—shorter series, but with an extra round of play. A three-game first round matchup and then division semi-finals and division finals that were five games apiece, and then, like the NHL, they had seven-game series. Two of them—one for the conference finals, and one for the Calder Cup.

Sixteen wins to the end.

That was like the big leagues.

And it was just brutal, a war of attrition to the ultimate prize.

I froze. Maybe that was what was happening in town, happening to me—a war of attrition until I fell apart. Well, I wasn't going to allow that to happen. And to prevent it, I needed caffeine. So, I grabbed my purse from the bottom drawer, walked out my office door, and, intent on my reinforcements of coffee and carbs, I nearly mowed Phoebe down.

"Shit," I said. "I'm sorry."

She rolled her eyes, but her mouth had softened, and her tone was laced with humor. "I see my apology made a really big difference, Billie Rose. Payback for the monkey bars?"

"Yup," I found myself joking back. "I decided to not be a mature adult and instead to attempt to tackle you at every opportunity—even though you're a good five inches taller than me."

"I wouldn't doubt your motivation." Her lips turned up. "You could take me."

I hitched my purse over my shoulder. "Yeah? You think so?"

Phoebe lifted her hands, seesawed them back and forth. "Maybe?"

"Ah, I see what this is about."

Phoebe lifted a brow.

"I ask no questions. You tell no lies."

"Exactly." And my former enemy laughed, and...I liked that, liked that we could get along enough to tell a couple of lame, nerdy jokes.

And it occurred to me that I could take this a little further, could keep moving forward.

"Can I buy you a cup of coffee?" I asked.

Phoebe went quiet, just for a second, and I was ready for her to snap back or to tell me to fuck off, or to act like the Phoebe I thought I'd known.

Instead, she said, "Yeah. I'd like that."

Progress.

We walked out of the Civic Center and around the corner for our sustenance, and as we came close to the front door of the coffee shop, I thought, *What the hell?* I might as well ask her.

"Is there a Roger Styles on your company's board?"

Phoebe froze, hand reaching for the door, eyes coming to mine. "Yes, he's the one who told me I needed to hire Willow."

My heart started pounding.

Jesus Fucking Christ.

"Really?"

She pulled open the door, held it for me. "Yeah," she said softly. "I'm sure. He's a real asshole. Kind of hard to forget. Why do you ask?"

"I just..." I bit the inside of my cheek and took a gamble. "I'm not sure how he fits in. We've been having some trouble in town that's not just the unexpected audit, and...well, his name has come up a lot."

"Trouble and Roger." She snorted. "Why doesn't that surprise me?" We started to move to the counter, then Phoebe drew to a halt, glancing back at me in concern. "What kind of trouble?"

"I don't think I should say," I told her. "Not yet. Not without understanding. I wouldn't want—" I shook my head, feeling guilty, not wanting her to think I was being a jerk who didn't want to confide in her. I just...couldn't risk it. "Especially if he's got power over you."

"Hey."

I glanced over at her.

Her expression was as gentle as her tone. "It's cool. I get it."

"I'm not trying to be a bitch. I just—"

"Billie." A bump of her shoulder against mine. "I get it."

I bit the inside of my cheek, whispered. "Thanks."

Phoebe smiled at me, and I moved to the counter, ordered, paid for our coffees (despite her protests), for two apple turnovers (also despite her protests), but it wasn't until we were heading for a table in the corner that something else occurred to me.

Something that might help me solve this once and for all.

"Phoebe?"

She'd pulled out a chair was halfway to sitting down in it, but paused, looked up at me, hovering above that wooden seat. "Yeah?"

"You don't have a picture of Roger, do you?"

FORTY

JOEL

"Gonna be a long one this morning, boys," Kenny called as we all queued up for the bus. "The fog is shit."

Our luggage was stored, some equipment was still being loaded, sticks and equipment and the like, but now it was time to get the hockey players on board.

The playoffs were beginning.

I turned to my dad, who was heading off to the airport and back home for Emma's dance recital, after he saw me off. "Thanks again for coming up."

"Sorry it was so short," he said, hugging me tight and thumping me on the back.

It *had* been a short visit, two days and one night, just a quick popover, but that he was willing to do it meant a lot. Hell, it meant everything.

"When the season's over, Rosie and I will come down," I promised, stepping back.

"I know." My dad laughed at what was probably my confused expression. "Rosie and Emma made a promise for a planning party.

Apparently, your woman has a subscription for a sticker company."

That was new information—the planning party *and* the sticker subscription—but it didn't surprise me. Neither of them did, really. "Well," I told him, "I guess I'll be third wheeling it."

My dad laughed, hugged me again, and then, with wishes of good luck and promises to talk to me soon, headed for his car, pulling out of the lot with a wave. He had a flight to catch, and I appreciated the send-off, even if I did wish Rosie had come to lay one on me.

I got that she was trying to give me time with my dad.

But I missed my kiss.

Though, not the hard-on that I dealt with for hours afterward, so maybe her not being here was a win?

No. No fucking way.

"Stop mooning for your mayor, Joey boy!" Fox called. "She's too busy doing real work to send you off with kisses!"

I flipped him off, hating that was all too close to what I'd been thinking.

But I started heading toward the bus anyway, watching as Fox clapped Kenny on the shoulder, hearing him say, "You'll get us there safely, Ken," he said. "You always do." Then he disappeared onto the bus, Ryan and some of the other guys following.

Right.

Time to go.

I tossed my messenger bag onto my shoulder, started to walk forward—

"Joel?"

The voice was quiet, hesitant...and determined.

I turned to see my Rosie's mom standing about ten feet behind me, clutching the strap of her purse and looking like she was going to run off into the pale sunshine of the obscenely early morning.

"Annie," I said, moving toward her, seeing that her skin was pale and her eyes were wild. "Are you all right?"

"I—" She cleared her throat, clutched the strap tighter. "I need to talk to you."

Well, fuck.

"I don't—" I cut my gaze back toward the bus, saw that mostly everyone was loaded on. "I don't really have a lot of time."

Her knuckles were white. Her eyes worried.

But she didn't turn and run, like I half expected.

Instead, her chin came up, her voice steadied, and she moved closer. "I need to talk to you about Rosie. I-it's important."

Maybe it was an asshole move, but once those words had hit my ears, I knew I'd make the bus wait for an eternity to hear what this woman wanted to tell me. "What?" I asked. "What do you need to tell me?"

Her lips pressed flat.

Released.

I channeled patience.

Luckily, I was getting really good at that. A skill I'd developed over the last weeks and months.

Yay for my not-so-ex wife appearing out of nowhere?

Hashtag life skills.

But even with that inner tangent, I was still waiting for Annie to speak.

"Mrs. Donovan," I murmured. "I don't want to be a jerk, but I really need you to just get to the point. The bus is getting ready to leave, which means there're dozens of people waiting for me right now to finish this conversation."

"Oh." Her gaze flicked behind me, presumably toward the waiting bus. "It's about Rosie."

"You said that," I pressed gently. "What about Rosie?"

"The trouble in town...it's not Rosie's fault. She didn't do anything wrong."

I knew that, but I didn't say it, just asked, "Okay, so whose fault is it?"

Panic in her eyes for a brief moment before her gaze dropped to the floor. "I know my Rosie," she said, voice barely audible. "I know she wouldn't do anything wrong."

"I know her too." I touched her arm, managed to get her gaze to come back up to mine. "I know her. I *love* her."

Annie jerked slightly.

"I know she would never do something that would hurt this town or her people. I know she would do it following the rules."

An image of Axel buck ass naked and calling for a ride flashed into my mind.

Because Rosie had brought his drunk ass to Bailey's porch and handcuffed him to the banister. Twice.

I amended my statement mentally.

She would follow the important rules. Meanwhile, something like kidnapping a drunk asshole who was tearing through her town might be on the table.

But the audit...they wouldn't find anything wrong on her end.

She'd lived on a fucking couch for months because she'd used her salary to help the town, to help people buy food and pay bills and rebuild in the aftermath of the fire. She hadn't even asked for reimbursement.

Because she'd had a shower in the ice rink and a place to sleep and food.

So, I knew she wasn't fucking around with money, wasn't taking it away from the people who needed it, and I'd heard her lament about the fucking policies and procedures that went into issuing one damned check often enough to know she followed them.

The audit would turn up nothing.

The petitions could go either way—the town might get fired up about the soccer tournament or the library books or the water conservation efforts. But the proper process would be followed, people's voices would be heard, and a decision would be made, one that might mean some of the residents weren't happy and others were.

That was fucking democracy.

But my Rosie lived and breathed for this town...

Which was why the recall was such a fucking kick in the teeth. That someone had filed the paperwork to start the process, that people might actually support it...after all she'd done for River's Bend—

I was furious *for* her.

I was—

"She would follow the rules," Annie whispered, and I refocused. "She's a good girl. She's always been a good girl. Even as a baby, she would hardly cry. Not like Bill—"

I watched the change slide over her like fog creeping into the hills surrounding the bay, sneaking fingers clouding the sky, darkening the present...and in Annie's case, drawing her back behind that blank shield.

"Annie," I said, lightly touching her shoulder.

A jerk.

A step back.

"I-I can't—" She shook her head. "Billy. John—" Another stuttering step backward.

"No"—I moved toward her, gently prying her hands free of her purse—"Not John. Not Billy. *Rosie*. What did you come here to tell me about *Rosie?*"

Her eyes cleared, just for a moment. "John," she whispered. "John *hates* her, and he would do anything to make her life miserable."

"I—"

Then she was yanking her hands free and sprinting across the parking lot.

I didn't chase her, just watched her drive away.

Then I got on the bus.

"Everything okay?" Ry asked.

"No," I said softly, pulling out my phone as the bus trundled forward and jabbing at the screen.

It rang twice before Rosie answered. "You just couldn't leave without hearing my voice, could you?" she teased.

Fuck. I loved that.

I loved her.

And I hated that I had to tell her this.

"Sweetheart," I said gently.

Instant alertness. "What's wrong?"

"Your mom was just here and she..."

Forty-One

BILLIE ROSE

I sat back in my office chair early the next morning, having stayed up way too late trying to find any sort of connection between my dad and the petitions.

And got nada.

He was a royal asshole and had standards I'd never be able to live up to, but I didn't have any evidence he was trying to ruin my life and career—

Any more than normal anyway.

Okay, that wasn't fair, I supposed.

He was the one to push me to do this job, to work my ass off for it, and to *keep* doing it.

Sighing, I rubbed at my face, probably smearing the makeup I'd so painstakingly applied that morning in an effort to hide the fact that I'd been up late researching and thinking and then tossing and turning in bed until the sun hit the horizon.

The only benefit was that I'd been up for the text Joel had sent, telling me he had arrived safely in the hotel.

A drive that had taken twice as long as normal because of the fog.

It was crazy thick and there had been several accidents, so knowing he and the guys were good, were heading to bed and prepping for the game the next day was a relief.

Not that it had helped *me* sleep.

I'd just...it was one worry I'd been able to put aside so I could focus on others.

Roger Styles, though, had stayed on my mind.

Phoebe had described him as tall and broad with blue eyes and dirty blond hair, but it wasn't like that description helped me narrow it down all that much. There were a couple of hundred men in River's Bend with that description, including my father, and that was assuming Roger was a resident. He could be someone I'd slighted in the past, someone who hated my father and decided to take it out on me. He could be some incel who'd seen me all over TV and social media and had money, power, and now a vendetta against me.

"Great, Billie," I muttered, shoving my hair back and checking my inbox for the umpteenth time since the coffee sit down with Phoebe yesterday. She hadn't had any pictures of Roger on her phone or in the cloud, but her administrative assistant had some headshots she was waiting on approval for.

Headshots Roger had been very difficult to tie down on— canceling appointments and no-showing with the photographer.

Which had started a little niggle in the back of my mind, an assurance that this was the path to continue on, to flesh out and track down. Roger was the key to all of this shit. I was sure of it... and now I just needed to wait until Phoebe's admin went into the office that morning and sent Roger's pictures to Phoebe.

Who would then send them to me.

So...I was sitting at my desk, twiddling my thumbs, diving deep on a shit-ton of random government sites and social media platforms I hadn't heard of and was organizing my notes on what I'd found and—

I stilled.

Frowned.

Leaned closer to my screen.

"What the fuck is that?" I whispered.

We worked in a cloud system, something that had protected us when the fire burned all our records, because most of our day-to-day operations were stored safely in servers away from the flames. The program was simple, akin to something like Google docs, except that it was secure, obviously.

Hopefully.

Maybe not?

Because the edit history on the right side of the page was...*off*?

An edit had been made when I wasn't here? Last night at three in the morning, when I'd been tossing and turning in bed, I'd supposedly deleted several bullet points.

"What the fuck?"

I clicked over to another file, this one my notes on the water conservation guidelines, something I hadn't touched in more than a week because of the other shit I was dealing with.

And there it was.

An edit from me, supposedly from two nights ago.

I frowned, trying to think up scenarios where this could actually make sense—maybe when I booted up my computer the edits processed or something? Which...*no*, that didn't make sense. It was all online, and I'd definitely been online at my computer between last week and two nights ago.

And—I thought back—I was pretty sure I'd forgotten to shut my computer down because when I came in yesterday, it had been on and running and—

"Hell," I muttered, rubbing my forehead. I couldn't be sure, but I grabbed my planner, wrote all of that down—on paper, because if the system was messed up then I was going old school.

Then I found a file I'd been given access to, because I had access to a lot of things, but one I *knew* I'd never so much as opened.

Because I had good people who ran the grant application program for a local scholarship for me. Good, experienced people who made the decisions for funding approvals that I only signed off on.

Something worthwhile my dad had taught me—one of the few things.

If I had good people working under me, I could get a lot more done.

But my heart sank when I opened the document.

Because...apparently, I'd made edits on this one too.

"What the hell?" I whispered, picking up the phone on my desk and hitting the line for Bella before realizing, as it rang and rang, that she wouldn't be in the office yet. "Damn," I muttered, setting the receiver back in the cradle and wondering when was the last time the password had been changed.

I tried to think back to who had trained me.

And...was it Bella? My dad? One of the engineers?

I couldn't remember.

My inbox pinged, and I clicked back to it, saw that Phoebe had emailed the photo I asked for.

"Finally," I whispered, knowing that wasn't fair, but also feeling like every single one of my nerves was tense, waiting.

Knowing this would change everything.

I scrolled down to the attachment, clicked, and—

A knock at my open door—I hadn't bothered to close it, considering it was just me in the office—had me looking up and away from my screen.

And frowning.

It was still early, so it was strange to see Mason—the city's attorney—standing in the opening, hesitating on the threshold, his expression stark. "You got a minute?"

"Of course," I said, waving him in to one of the chairs at the front of my desk. "What's up?"

He didn't reply, just stepped into my office.

I glanced back to my screen, saw the photograph had finally loaded, and froze, went utterly, statue still.

What the fuck?

What *the fuck?*

That was—

I blinked, leaned closer, confirming that my eyes were seeing what I was seeing, that there weren't mushrooms or something in my coffee that was making me hallucinate that...

Roger Styles was...*my dad.*

Only I didn't have time to confirm that, *to process that*... because Mason wasn't alone as he walked into my office.

And it wasn't until I saw who was behind him that I knew.

Knew that everything I worked so fucking hard for was about to implode.

Because Dave, the police chief, wearing his full uniform and an expression that was severe, had followed Mason into the room.

And he was unclipping his cuffs, striding toward me.

"You have the right to remain silent..."

———

EEK! I hope you love being on this journey with Joel and Rosie as much as I do! The next book in their Rush Hockey trilogy is NO PUCKS LOST BETWEEN US. **I had a love-hate relationship with hockey players...**

CLICK HERE TO READ NO PUCKS LOST BETWEEN US NOW>

———

If you enjoy my series, considering supporting me on PATREON! Get access to early releases, bonus content, character art, audiobooks, and much more!

CLICK HERE TO SUPPORT ME>

———

And if you enjoyed ALL'S FAIR IN PUCKS AND WAR, you'll love the sexy, sweet, and close-knit Breakers Hockey crew. It's full of hot hockey players, cinnamon roll heroes, and found family! The first book in the series, BROKEN, is now live!

"It is sexy, hot, adorable and such a fun read. You will not be able to put this down!" —Amazon Reviewer

———

I so appreciate your help in spreading the word about my books, including sharing with friends! Please leave a review on your favorite book site!

You can also join my Facebook group, the Fabinators, for exclusive giveaways and sneak peeks of future books.

SIGN UP FOR ELISE FABER'S NEWSLETTER HERE: https://www.elisefaber.com/newsletter

Rush Hockey

Big Puck Energy
Filthy Puckboy
So Pucking Over It
Love, Pucks, and Other Stories
All's Fair in Pucks and War
No Pucks Lost Between Us

————

Hate missing Elise's new releases? Love contests, exclusive excerpts and giveaways?
Then signup for Elise's newsletter here!
www.elisefaber.com/newsletter

————

If you enjoy my series, considering supporting me on PATREON!
Get access to early releases, bonus content, character art, audiobooks, and much more!
CLICK HERE TO SUPPORT ME>

————

And join Elise's fan group, the Fabinators (https://www.facebook.com/groups/fabinators) for insider information, sneak peaks at new releases, and fun freebies! Hope to see you there!

————

Also by Elise Faber

Billionaire's Club (all stand alone)

Bad Night Stand

Bad Breakup

Bad Husband

Bad Hookup

Bad Divorce

Bad Fiancé

Bad Boyfriend

Bad Blind Date

Bad Wedding

Bad Engagement

Bad Bridesmaid

Bad Swipe

Bad Girlfriend

Bad Best Friend

Bad Billionaire's Quickies

Gold Hockey (all stand alone)

Blocked

Backhand

Boarding

Benched

Breakaway

Breakout

Checked

Coasting

Centered

Charging

Caged

Crashed

A Gold Christmas

Cycled

Caught

Cap

Covered

Crushed

Changed

Breakers Hockey (all stand alone)

<u>Broken</u>

<u>Boldly</u>

<u>Breathless</u>

<u>Ballsy</u>

Rush Hockey Trilogy #1

Big Puck Energy

Filthy Puckboy

So Pucking Over It

Rush Hockey Trilogy #2

Love, Pucks, and Other Stories

All's Fair in Pucks and War

No Pucks Left Behind

Love, Action, Camera (all stand alone)

Dotted Line

Action Shot

Close-Up

End Scene

Meet Cute

Love After Midnight (all stand alone)

Rum And Notes

Virgin Daiquiri

On The Rocks

Sex On The Seats

Life Sucks Series (all stand alone)

Train Wreck

Hot Mess

Dumpster Fire

Clusterf*@k

FUBAR

Perfect Storm

Free Fall

Lost Cause

Roosevelt Ranch Series (all stand alone, series complete)

Disaster at Roosevelt Ranch

Heartbreak at Roosevelt Ranch

Collision at Roosevelt Ranch

Regret at Roosevelt Ranch

Desire at Roosevelt Ranch

Phoenix Series (read in order)

Phoenix Rising

Dark Phoenix

Phoenix Freed

Phoenix: LexTal Chronicles (rereleasing soon, stand alone, Phoenix world)

From Ashes

In Flames

To Smoke

KTS Series (all stand alone, series complete)

Riding The Edge

Crossing The Line

Leveling The Field

Scorching The Earth

Cocky Heroes World

Tattooed Troublemaker

About the Author

USA Today bestselling author, Elise Faber, loves chocolate, Star Wars, Harry Potter, and hockey (the order depending on the day and how well her team -- the Sharks! -- are playing). She and her husband also play as much hockey as they can squeeze into their schedules, so much so that their typical date night is spent on the ice. Elise is the mom to two exuberant boys and lives in Northern California. Connect with her in her Facebook group, the Fabinators or find more information about her books at www.elise-faber.com.

facebook.com/elisefaberauthor

amazon.com/author/elisefaber

bookbub.com/profile/elise-faber

instagram.com/elisefaber

tiktok.com/@elisefaberauthor

goodreads.com/elisefaber